## Dedica

*To the nuclear test veterans around the world,*
*who have suffered for too long*

*We will never forget each and every one of you.*

*For those families who are suffering genetic illnesses linked to*
*the aforementioned British nuclear tests*

*Live every day as if it were your last. One day you will be right.*

50% of profits from every book sold will be donated to the
British Nuclear Test Veterans Association
Registered Charity No. 1173575

# Contents

# Introduction

Firstly, let me introduce myself. My name is James Gordon Josephson and I am now 98 years old. I was born in London in 1920 and spent my working life as a civil servant working for the UK government.

I never married and have no children or any family members, so this account of my life is something I have wanted to do for several years. I can no longer live with the guilt and the betrayal of my fellow UK citizens and their families.

I have been diagnosed with terminal cancer (lung) and I have a few months left to live. I hope this account of events relating to the British nuclear tests will be used by the BNTVA to claim compensation from the UK government and will stop the lies and betrayals.

This account has been written by Slaine McRoth, an independent journalist who has sat and listened to me since January 2018.

My working life has been dedicated to serving this great nation. I am proud to have served in the Second World War and to have served as a civil servant until my retirement aged 65. Since my retirement I have also been retained as a consultant due to my knowledge of the nuclear tests. I have tried to include as much information relating to each test as possible without detailing too many technical details.

I spent my National Service in the army, in the Logistics Corp. I did not travel abroad due to my asthma condition, but my degree in Engineering was used within the army to ensure that reports were correctly formatted and were accurate.

This account of my life is not about me personally; it is about my involvement in the nuclear testing programme and the cover up that has continued until this present day. I had very high security clearance within the MoD and the documents that I have both written and read will never be released as they contain evidence of a conspiracy with unbelievable consequences.

I understand that when this document is published, I will be breaking the Official Secrets Act and I could be tried for treason, but I am a sick man and I do not believe I will be alive by the time this document is released to the public.

Mr McRoth and I have not disclosed this story to anyone else or consulted any other person. This is my story and whilst it may seem like an episode of the US TV Show 'The X Files', I can assure you that it is real life and I am ashamed to be part of it.

# Chapter 1 - Background Information

The UK initiated a nuclear weapons programme, codenamed Tube Alloys, during the Second World War. At the Quebec Conference in August 1943, it was merged with the American Manhattan Project. The British contribution to the Manhattan Project saw British scientists participate in most of its work. The British government considered nuclear weapons to be a joint discovery, but the American Atomic Energy Act of 1946 (McMahon Act) restricted other countries, including the UK, from access to information about nuclear weapons.

Fearing the loss of Britain's great power status, the UK resumed its own project, now codenamed High Explosive Research. On 3 October 1952, it detonated an atomic bomb in the Monte Bello Islands of Western Australia in Operation Hurricane. Eleven more British nuclear weapons tests in Australia were carried out over the following decade, including seven British nuclear tests at Maralinga in 1956 and 1957.

The British hydrogen bomb programme demonstrated Britain's ability to produce thermonuclear weapons in the Operation Grapple nuclear tests in the Pacific and led to the amendment of the McMahon Act.

Since the 1958 US-UK Mutual Defence Agreement, the US and the UK have cooperated extensively on nuclear security matters. The nuclear Special Relationship between the two countries has involved the exchange of classified scientific data and fissile materials such as uranium-235 and plutonium. In 1961-1963, British forces participated in Operation Dominic on Christmas Island.

The UK has not had a programme to develop an independent delivery system since the cancellation of the Blue Streak in 1960. Instead, it has purchased US delivery systems for UK use, fitting them with warheads designed and manufactured by the UK's Atomic Weapons Establishment (AWE) and its predecessor.

Under the 1963 Polaris Sales Agreement, the US supplied the UK with Polaris missiles and nuclear submarine technology. The US also supplied the RAF and British Army of the Rhine with nuclear weapons under Project E until 1992. Nuclear-capable American aircraft have been based in the UK since 1949, but the last US nuclear weapons were withdrawn in 2006.

My involvement comes at the very start of the whole sordid affair. I was present at the 1943 Quebec conference on secondment from the British Navy to publish reports on the conference and to provide minutes of the meetings.

If I could have one wish now, it would be that I had never attended the conference and that I had never heard of nuclear technology, let alone be involved in its development.

# Chapter 2 – Early Life

I spent time with the scientists on the Manhattan Project as a founder member of a secret department of the MoD called 'Nuclear Matters'. This department consisted of scientists, mathematicians, senior officials and representatives of the combined forces. This department was classified as top secret.

Apart from the senior officials, no one knew of the existence of this department and all information was highly classified. The Manhattan Project was my first experience of nuclear technology and the impact on the lives of the people who participated in the experiment.

I call it an experiment, because that is what it was. We were playing with the science: the theories needed to be proven and we were tasked with ensuring that they were, whatever the cost.

The Manhattan Project was a research and development undertaking during World War II that produced the first nuclear weapons. It was led by the United States with the support of the United Kingdom and Canada. From 1942 to 1946, the project was under the direction of Major General Leslie Groves of the US Army Corps of Engineers. Nuclear physicist Robert Oppenheimer was the director of the Los Alamos Laboratory that designed the actual bombs. The army component of the project was designated the Manhattan District; *Manhattan* gradually superseded the official codename, Development of Substitute Materials, for the entire project.

Along the way, the project absorbed its earlier British counterpart, Tube Alloys. The Manhattan Project began modestly in 1939 but grew to employ more than 130,000 people and cost nearly US $2 billion (about $22 billion in 2016[1] dollars). Over 90% of the cost was for building factories and to produce fissile material, with less than 10% for development and production of the weapons. Research and production took place at more than 30 sites across the United States, the United Kingdom, and Canada.

---

[1] https://en.wikipedia.org/wiki/Manhattan_Project#cite_note-inflation-USGDP-1

Two types of atomic bombs were developed concurrently during the war: a relatively simple gun-type fission weapon and a more complex implosion-type nuclear weapon. The Thin Man gun-type design proved impractical to use with plutonium, and therefore a simpler gun-type called Little Boy was developed that used uranium-235, an isotope that makes up only 0.7 per cent of natural uranium. Chemically identical to the most common isotope, uranium-238, and with almost the same mass, it proved difficult to separate the two. Three methods were employed for uranium enrichment: electromagnetic, gaseous and thermal. Most of this work was performed at the Clinton Engineer Works at Oak Ridge, Tennessee.

I spent most of my time in Tennessee, ensuring that the project was fully documented and reported back to the MoD.

In parallel with the work on uranium was an effort to produce plutonium. After the feasibility of the world's first artificial nuclear reactor was demonstrated in Chicago at the Metallurgical Laboratory, it designed the X-10 Graphite Reactor at Oak Ridge and the production reactors in Hanford, Washington, in which uranium was irradiated and transmuted into plutonium. The plutonium was then chemically separated from the uranium, using the bismuth phosphate process. The Fat Man plutonium implosion-type weapon was developed in a concerted design and development effort by the Los Alamos Laboratory.

I should be proud to say that I was present at the demonstration of the first artificial reactor, and I was at the time, but now some 75 years later, I am not.

The project was also charged with gathering intelligence on the German nuclear weapon project. Through Operation Alsos, Manhattan Project personnel served in Europe, sometimes behind enemy lines, where they gathered nuclear materials and documents, and rounded up German scientists. Despite the Manhattan Project's tight security, Soviet atomic spies successfully penetrated the programme.

My first encounter with espionage and the lengths to which governments would go was in 1944 when we discovered a Soviet spy within our ranks. He had been exposed to very sensitive information and was passing it to the Soviet Union on a regular basis. I was tasked with ensuring that this person was passed information that was incorrect and would lead to the Soviet Union constructing a device that would never function. Very important steps in the construction were omitted from the paperwork given to the spy.

This spy was then removed from his post one day and I never saw him again. Despite access to high level clearance and my own investigations, I will go to my grave not knowing what happened to him.

The first nuclear device ever detonated was an implosion-type bomb at the Trinity test, conducted at New Mexico's Alamogordo Bombing and Gunnery Range on 16 July 1945. This test was hailed a success but proved to be one of the 'dirtiest' bombs ever detonated. We had theories on the impact to the ground, air, sea and where the fallout would land, but we really had no idea what we were unleashing onto the world. We were treated to a fine meal and received bonus payments in our payroll that month. The scientists were delighted that their initial theories were correct and that they had finally detonated a nuclear device. If only we had known that it would be used so soon to devastating consequences.

Little Boy and Fat Man bombs were used a month later in the atomic bombings of Hiroshima and Nagasaki, respectively. We were initially horrified to see the images of the destruction to human life and the environment around the detonation site. What had we done? Our work had developed the most destructive device ever.

I was posted back to the UK and I believed that my involvement in the project had ceased, until March 1947 when I was again involved in the British testing programme.

In the immediate post-war years, the Manhattan Project conducted weapons testing at Bikini Atoll as part of Operation Crossroads, developed new weapons, promoted the development of the network of national laboratories, supported medical research into radiology and laid the foundations for the nuclear navy. It maintained control over American atomic weapons research and production until the formation of the United States Atomic Energy Commission in January 1947.

# Chapter 3 – Back in the UK

On returning to the UK, I attended a meeting of the 'Nuclear Matters Committee', or NMC as it was now known. The first item on the agenda was to ensure that the documents relating to the UK involvement in the Manhattan Project were stored securely, classified accordingly and not made available to any public body or person under any circumstances. Any freedom of information requests or court orders were to be fought in court at any cost.

Budgets were implemented to ensure that this procedure could be implemented for the next 100 years. Documents were to be stored in a secure location at the new GCHQ site being built in 1951. But for now, we were to use Bletchley Park.

We spent three years ensuring that the documents were correctly filed, classified and indexed. These documents contained extremely sensitive information, including designs for the devices from the Manhattan Project, reports on Hiroshima and Nagasaki and the effects. Few people knew the major effects of these detonations and the effect that it had on the population. Below is an extract from the documents:

*By August 1945, the Allies' Manhattan Project had produced two types of atomic bomb, and the 509th Composite Group of the United States Army Air Forces (USAAF) was equipped with the specialized Silverplate version of the Boeing B-29 Superfortress that could deliver them from Tinian in the Mariana Islands. Orders for atomic bombs to be used on four Japanese cities were issued on July 25.*

*On August 6, one of its B-29s dropped a Little Boy uranium gun-type bomb on Hiroshima. Three days later, on August 9, a Fat Man plutonium implosion-type bomb was dropped by another B-29 on Nagasaki. The bombs immediately devastated their targets.*

*Over the next two to four months, the acute effects of the atomic bombings killed 90,000–146,000 people in Hiroshima and 39,000–80,000 people in Nagasaki; roughly half of the deaths in each city occurred on the first day. Large numbers of people continued to die from the effects of burns, radiation sickness, and other injuries, compounded by illness and malnutrition, for many months afterward. In both cities, most of the dead were civilians, although Hiroshima had a sizable military garrison.*

*Japan announced its surrender to the Allies on August 15, six days after the bombing of Nagasaki and the Soviet Union's declaration of war. On September 2, the Japanese government signed the instrument of surrender, effectively ending World War II.*

The death toll from the technology that I had helped to create is something I have had to endure every day of my life. I thought that this would be the worst that humans could release on itself. Little did I know at the time that the UK government was preparing something much worse for the UK armed forces.

Safely secured in a vault in the depths of GCHQ, protected by classification and the highest access protocols, even restricted to the Prime Minister and unknown to the Queen, we kept the secret safe from any unwanted attention from the Soviet Union and Germany.

# Chapter 4 – High Explosive Research

High Explosive Research was a British project to independently develop atomic bombs after the Second World War. This decision was taken by a cabinet sub-committee on 8 January 1947, in response to apprehension of an American return to isolationism, fears that Britain might lose its great power status, and the actions by the United States to unilaterally withdraw from sharing of nuclear technology under the 1943 Quebec Agreement. The decision was publicly announced in the House of Commons on 12 May 1948.

I was again called to the cabinet sub-committee due to my work on the Manhattan Project. I was to now become one of the senior officials on the project, responsible for all documentation.

The project was a civil, not a military, one. Staff were drawn from and recruited into the Civil Service and were paid Civil Service salaries. It was headed by Lord Portal, as Controller of Production, Atomic Energy, in the Ministry of Supply. An Atomic Energy Research Establishment was located at a former airfield, Harwell, in Berkshire, under the direction of John Cockcroft. The first nuclear reactor in the UK, a small research reactor known as GLEEP, went critical at Harwell on 15 August 1947. British staff at the Montreal Laboratory designed a larger reactor, known as BEPO, which went critical on 5 July 1948. They provided experience and expertise that would later be employed on the larger production reactors.

My involvement was with both projects and once again I was at the forefront of the technology. These reactors were of poor design and we had no idea of the potential fallout at the time. Development of the reactors was still at an early stage.

Production facilities were constructed under the direction of Christopher Hinton, who established his headquarters in a former Royal Ordnance Factory at Risley in Lancashire. These included a uranium metal plant at Springfields, nuclear reactors and a plutonium processing plant at Windscale, and a gaseous diffusion uranium enrichment facility at Capenhurst, near Chester. The two Windscale reactors became operational in October 1950 and June 1951. The gaseous diffusion plant at Capenhurst began producing highly enriched uranium in 1954.

I spent my time between the sites, with various audits, discussions, meetings and production of documentation. My main role was to ensure that no information relating to these projects was released without the correct security clearance. We did not want any other country interfering with our technology.

William Penney directed bomb design from Fort Halstead. In 1951, his design group moved to a new site at Aldermaston in Berkshire. I was deployed to Aldermaston as it became the focal point for the development of a nuclear bomb.

Aldermaston was a fantastic place to be working; cutting edge technology and the development of further technology excited the scientists. We had unlimited budgets, the backing of the government, and we could ask for anything we required and clearance would be granted. The budget for the development seemed endless.

William Penney was a brilliant scientist; his vision and development skills were fascinating to watch. He was dedicated to his work and was desperate to prove his theories.

# Chapter 5 – The Start of the Experiment

William Penney had completed his development, the bomb was ready, and the theories now needed to be tested in a real-life environment.

I was called to a meeting of the Nuclear Matters Committee (NMC) in Aldermaston to decide where the bomb could be detonated. This meeting was a debate on the least populated area away from the UK where a bomb could be exploded, and the outcomes of the test could be documented and analysed.

Various sites were debated. The UK had control of several remote islands across the world and each one was discussed in turn, including Christmas Island and the Montebello Islands. Each location was to be analysed for population, the ground structure, the wind and several environmental factors. Cost was never considered during the choice of the islands.

The study noted several requirements for a test area:

- an isolated area with no human habitation for 100 miles (160 km) downwind;
- large enough to accommodate a dozen detonations over a period of several years;
- prevailing winds that would blow fallout out to sea but away from shipping lanes;
- a temporary camp site at least 10 miles (16 km) upwind of the detonation area;
- a base camp site at least 25 miles (40 km) upwind of the detonation area, with room for laboratories, workshops and signals equipment;
- ready for use by mid-1952.

The first test would probably be a ground burst, but consideration was also given to an explosion in a ship to measure the effect of a ship-borne atomic bomb on a major port. Such data would complement that obtained about an underwater explosion by the American Operation Crossroads nuclear test in 1946 and would therefore be of value to the

Americans. Seven Canadian sites were assessed, the most promising being Churchill, Manitoba, but the waters were too shallow to allow ships to approach close to shore.

It was at this meeting that the first discussions took place relating to the armed forces personnel involved. This meeting was the start of the 100-year monitoring experiment and the biggest human experiment ever undertaken by the British Government.

It was decided at this meeting that the following would be undertaken:

- All UK armed forces personnel involved would be tagged for life.
- All UK armed forces would be chosen from healthy male personnel and would ideally be single.
- Senior officials and scientific officers would wear protective clothing and would be removed as far away as possible from the proximity of the detonations.
- Personnel on the ground, within ships and aircraft classified as within the proximity of the detonations would be tagged and monitored for radiation using film badges and logged accordingly.
- Animals would also be exposed to the tests, including rabbits, dogs and mice.
- The monitoring of the armed forces personnel would continue after the tests, until the death of the individual.
- The monitoring of the armed forces personnel's families, including widows, children and grandchildren, would continue until 2050.

I was astounded to listen to the meeting and to document the fact that the UK government was prepared to use its own military personnel as guinea pigs, not just at the tests but to monitor the effects until 2050. While the location of the test site was still to be decided, the motion to monitor the military personnel was passed and I was tasked with setting up the internal monitoring systems within the various government departments. A big task!

The preferred site was the Pacific Proving Grounds in the US-controlled Marshall Islands. As a fall-back, sites in Canada and Australia were considered. The Admiralty suggested that the Montebello Islands, 80 miles (130 km) off the Pilbara coast of north-western Australia, might be suitable so the Prime Minister of the United Kingdom, Clement Attlee, sent a request to the Prime Minister of Australia, Robert Menzies. Limited in natural fuel reserves, Australia was interested in exploring atomic energy as well as nuclear weapons, so with hopes of a UK-Australia collaboration in mind, permission was granted for a survey of the islands to take place.

The three-man survey party, headed by Air Vice Marshal E. D. Davis, arrived in Sydney on 1 November 1950, and embarked on HMAS *Karangi*, under the command of Commander A. H. Cooper, who carried out a detailed hydrographic survey of the islands. The charts at the Admiralty had been made by HMS *Beagle* in August 1840. Soundings were taken of the depths of coastal waters to measure the tides, and samples of the gravel and sand were taken to assess whether they could be used for making concrete. The work afloat and ashore was complemented by Royal Australian Air Force (RAAF) aerial photography of the islands. The British survey team returned to London on 29 November 1950. The islands were assessed as suitable for atomic testing, but, for climatic reasons, only in October. HMAS *Karangi* was used as a survey ship

On 27 March 1951, Attlee sent Menzies a personal message saying that, while negotiations with the United States site were ongoing, work would need to begin if the Montebello Islands were to be used the following October. Menzies replied that he could not authorise the test until after the Australian federal election, to be held on 28 April 1951, but was willing to allow work to continue. Menzies was re-elected, and the Australian government formally agreed in May 1951. On 28 May, Attlee sent a comprehensive list of assistance that he hoped Australia would provide. A more detailed survey was requested, which was carried out by HMAS *Warrego* in July and August 1951. The British government emphasised the importance of security, so not to imperil its negotiations with the United States. The Australian government gave all weapon design data a classification of "Top Secret", with all other aspects of the test being "Classified". Nuclear weapons design was already covered by a D-Notice in the United Kingdom. Australian D Notice No. 8 was issued to cover nuclear tests.

Meanwhile, negotiations continued with the Americans. Oliver Franks, the British Ambassador to the United States, lodged a formal request on 2 August 1951 for use of the Nevada Test Site. This was looked upon favourably by the United States Secretary of State, Dean Acheson, and the chairman of the United States Atomic Energy Commission, Gordon Dean, but opposed by Robert A. Lovett, the Deputy Secretary of Defense, and Robert LeBaron, the Deputy Secretary of Defense for Atomic Energy Affairs.

The British government had announced on 7 June 1951 that Donald Maclean, who had served as a British member of the Combined Policy Committee from January 1947 to August 1948, had been a Soviet spy. In view of security concerns, Lovett and LeBaron wanted the tests to be conducted by Americans, with British participation limited to Penney and a few selected British scientists. Truman endorsed this counterproposal on 24 September 1951.

The Nevada Test Site would be cheaper than Montebello, although the cost would be paid in scarce dollars. Information gathered would have to be shared with the Americans, who would not share their own data. It would not be possible to test from a ship, and the political advantages in demonstrating that Britain could develop and test nuclear weapons without American assistance would be foregone. The Americans were under no obligation to make the test site available for subsequent tests. Also, as Lord Cherwell noted, an American test meant that "in the lamentable event of the bomb failing to detonate, we should look very foolish indeed."

A final decision was deferred until after the 1951 election. This resulted in a change of government, with the Conservative Party returning to power and Churchill replacing Attlee as Prime Minister. On 27

December 1951, the High Commissioner of the United Kingdom to Australia informed Menzies of the British government's decision to use Montebello.

On 26 February 1952, Churchill announced in the House of Commons that the first British atomic bomb test would occur in Australia before the end of the year. When queried by a Labour Party backbencher, Emrys Hughes, about the impact on the local flora and fauna, Churchill joked that the survey team had only seen some birds and lizards. Among the AERE scientists was an amateur biologist, Frank Hill, who collected samples of the flora and fauna on the islands, teaming up with Commander G. Wedd, who collected marine specimens from the surrounding waters. In a paper published by the Linnean Society of London, Hill catalogued over 400 species of plants and animals. This included 20 new species of insects, six of plants, and a new species of legless lizard.

# Chapter 6 – Monitoring the Personnel

As I walked away from that initial meeting, I had a moral dilemma: should I remain in post? This was to be a human experiment using the deadliest technology ever developed. Could this really be happening? What would happen if I decided I no longer wanted to be involved? I already knew about the experiment and the potential consequences (or so I thought).

I dd not sleep well that night and for several nights after the meeting. Everyone was very busy with the preparations for the test on the Montebello Islands; the plans were being drawn up and the military personnel were already being selected.

I needed to develop a system which would 'tag' any participant in the test so any medical records, military records, marriages, divorces, births of children, deaths of children and deaths of the personnel themselves were immediately flagged to our department so we could analyse the findings and, if necessary, attend operations, meet with physicians and any government representatives.

This monitoring needed to be set up without the knowledge of the personnel or their families and we would need to educate anyone involved in their medical lives.

This was a huge task. We did not have computer systems in those days; everything was paper-based, and records of operations were sometimes not correctly documented, especially within the armed forces.

The tagging needed to be across the combined forces, and it had to encompass their whole lives and the lives of their families.

I headed up a team of civil servants who deliberated for weeks on the best solution to our problem.

Our main issue was that we did not know if this was to be the only test, or if the tests would continue in the future. How many personnel were to be involved? Hundreds? Thousands? The scale of the experiment was unknown to us.

We decided to tag the military records of each person involved in the tests with a NP flag, which stood for 'Nuclear Participant'. We then categorised them further depending on their role within the test and the exposure levels that were relevant to their job role. Exposure levels were from 1-10. In our system, a pilot flying through the mushroom cloud would be classified as a NP1.

We now had to find the personnel to be involved in the tests.

# Chapter 7 – Finding Personnel

The heads of the three services were called to a meeting of the NMC to discuss the exercise and the detonation of the device on Montebello.

It was to be a combined forces operation with personnel needed to prepare the site, deliver the equipment and ensure the tests ran smoothly with little or no media relating to the test.

Personnel were to be chosen by their commanding officers and the full range of personnel were required. Codenamed Operation Hurricane, the date of the test was set for 3 October 1952. We did not have long to prepare.

- Personnel were to be chosen based on the following factors:
- No existing medical conditions
- Single
- Under 24 years old
- Male
- No children (where possible)

Requests were put out to volunteers to take part in Operation Hurricane. The personnel were not aware of the detonation at this time, just an overseas operation to the Montebello Islands. Most of the personnel had never heard of the Montebello Islands and most had certainly never visited them.

We were given the personnel list, containing full details of their medical status and role, which meant we could now classify the personnel with our new NP grading system.

All personnel involved in the tests were checked medically and samples of their blood were taken and analysed. (DNA testing was not invented yet as we did not have the technology to record it.)

The personnel become the first entries into our new filing system and were known to us as the Originators. These men were to form the basis of the experiment and we used their files as test files for our new system.

Each file was listed under their service number, given a NP ranking and contained their basic details, medical details and blood sample analysis. Height, weight, skin conditions, heart, teeth, lung capacity, eye sight, hearing and kidney function were all recorded.

The NP flag was also attached to their military records and their civilian medical records, and the births, deaths and marriages log was also updated with the flag to ensure we would be alerted to any new entries.

Because of the proximity of the islands to Australia, representatives of the Australian Royal Navy were also present at the tests, and details of these personnel were also kept by the NMC.

Personnel from my section were also sent to the islands as part of the scientific team to ensure that the documentation was collated and kept secure. Due to my senior rank, I was not to be part of this team during the tests, but I would oversee them from afar.

# Chapter 8 – Operation Hurricane: Preparation

To coordinate the test, codenamed Operation Hurricane, the British government established a Hurricane Executive Committee chaired by the Deputy Chief of the Naval Staff, Vice Admiral Edward Evans-Lombe. It held its first meeting in May 1951. I was present at this meeting to ensure that the results and the monitoring of the personnel would be completed successfully.

To deal with it, an Australian Hurricane Panel was created, chaired by the Australian Deputy Chief of the Naval Staff, Captain Alan McNicoll. Its other members were Colonel John Wilton from the Australian Army, Group Captain Alister Murdoch from the RAAF and Charles Spry from the Australian Security Intelligence Organisation (ASIO). A pressing question was that of observers. Churchill decided to exclude the media and members of the UK parliament. Canadian scientists and technicians would have access to all technical data, but Australians would not. I was to have full access to all data to ensure that full personnel monitoring was completed. This gave me the highest level of clearance for the tests.

Penney was anxious to secure the services of Ernest William Titterton, a British nuclear physicist who had recently emigrated to Australia, as he had worked on the American Trinity and Crossroads tests. Menzies asked the vice chancellor of the Australian National University, Sir Douglas Copland, to release Titterton to work on Operation Hurricane. Cockcroft also wanted assistance from Leslie Martin, the Department of Defence's Science Advisor, who was also a professor of physics at the University of Melbourne, to work in the health physics area. The two men knew each other from their time at Cambridge University before the war. After some argument, Martin was accepted as an official observer, as was W. A. S. Butement, the Chief Scientist at the Department of Supply. The only other official observer was Omond Solandt, a renowned scientist from Canada.

An advance party of No. 5 Airfield Construction Squadron from RAAF Base Williamtown, New South Wales, moved to Onslow in

August 1951 with heavy construction equipment, taking the train to Geraldton and then the road to Onslow. This was then transported to the Montebello Islands. A prefabricated hut was taken across by *Karangi*, along with equipment for establishing a meteorological station. Other material was moved from Onslow to the islands in 40-measurement-ton (45 m$^3$) lots in an ALC-40 landing craft manned by the Australian Army and towed by *Karangi*. This included two 25-ton bulldozers, a grader, tip trucks, portable generators, 400-imperial-gallon (1,800 l) water tanks and a mobile radio transceiver. The hut was erected, and the meteorological station henceforth manned by an RAAF officer and four assistants. Roads and landings were constructed, and camp sites established.

The next stage of work began in February 1952, in the wake of the December decision to proceed with the test. A detachment of No. 5 Airfield Construction Squadron was flown to Onslow from RAAF Bankstown in two RAAF Dakota aircraft and were then taken to the islands by the *Bathurst*-class corvette HMAS *Mildura*. *Karangi* fetched 90 measurement tons (100 m$^3$) of Marston Mat from Darwin that was used for road works and hardstands. The SS *Dorrigo* brought in another 90 measurement tons (100 m$^3$) three weeks later.

A water supply was also developed. To bring water from the Fortescue River, a quantity of 4-inch (100 mm) Victaulic-coupling pipe was brought from the Department of Works in Sydney and the Woomera Rocket Range in South Australia. Because the pipe was laid around obstacles, this proved to be insufficient. No more pipe was in storage, so a firm in Melbourne was asked to make some. An order was placed on a Friday evening, and the pipe was shipped the following Thursday morning, making its way to the Fortescue River by road and rail. The system delivered up to 3,400 imperial gallons (15,000 l) per hour to a jetty on the Fortescue estuary, from which it was taken to the islands by the 120ft Motor Lighter *MWL 251*.

The British assembled a small fleet for Operation Hurricane that included the escort carrier HMS *Campania*, which served as the flagship, and the Landing Ship Tanks (LSTs) *Narvik*, *Zeebrugge* and

*Tracker*, under the command of Rear Admiral A. D. Torlesse. Leonard Tyte from Aldermaston was appointed the technical director. *Campania* had five aircraft embarked, three Westland WS-51 Dragonfly helicopters and two Supermarine Sea Otter amphibians. Between them, the LSTs carried five LCMs and twelve LCAs (mechanized and amphibious landing craft).

The bomb, less its radioactive components, was assembled at Foulness, and then taken to the River-class frigate HMS *Plym* on 5 June 1952 for transportation to Australia. It took *Campania* and *Plym* eight weeks to make the voyage, as they sailed around the Cape of Good Hope instead of traversing the Suez Canal because there was unrest in Egypt at the time.

The Montebello Islands were reached on 8 August. *Plym* was anchored in 39 feet (12 m) of water, 1,150 feet (350 m) off Trimouille Island. The radioactive components, the plutonium core and polonium-beryllium neutron initiator went by air, flying from RAF Lyneham to Singapore in Handley Page Hastings aircraft via Cyprus, Sharjah and Ceylon. From Singapore they made the final leg of their journey in a Short Sunderland flying boat.

The British bomb design was like that of the American Fat Man, but for reasons of safety and efficiency the British design incorporated a levitated pit in which there was an air gap between the uranium tamper and the plutonium core. This gave the explosion time to build up momentum, similar in principle to a hammer hitting a nail, enabling less plutonium to be used. This design was an enhancement on the Fat Man design and was seen as a breakthrough in nuclear weapon technology at the time.

The British fleet was joined by eleven Royal Australian Navy (RAN) ships, including the aircraft carrier HMAS *Sydney* with 805 and 817 Squadrons embarked, and its four escorts: the destroyer HMAS *Tobruk* and frigates *Shoalhaven*, *Macquarie* and *Murchison*. For safety and security reasons, a prohibited area was declared around the islands. The Defence (Special Undertakings) Act (1952) was quickly passed through the Parliament of Australia between 4 and 6 June 1952 and received assent on 10 June. Under the new act, everything within a 45-mile (72 km) radius of Flag Island was declared a prohibited area. That some of this was outside Australia's 3-mile (4.8 km) territorial waters attracted comment. The frigate HMAS *Hawkesbury* was tasked with patrolling the prohibited area, while its sister ship HMAS *Culgoa* acted as a weather ship. Logistical support was provided by HMAS *Warreen*, *Limicola* and *Mildura*, the motor water lighter *MWL 251* and the motor refrigeration lighter *MRL 252*, and the tugboat HMAS *Reserve*, which towed a fuel barge. Dakotas of No. 86 Wing RAAF provided air patrols and a weekly courier run.

# Chapter 9 – Operation Hurricane

The main site, known as H1, was established on Hermite Island. This was the location of the control room from which the bomb would be detonated, along with the equipment to monitor the firing circuits and telemetry. It was also the location of the generators that provided electric power, and recharged the batteries of portable devices, and ultra-high-speed cameras operating at up to 8,000 frames per second.

Other camera equipment was set up on Alpha Island and Northwest Island. Most of the monitoring equipment was positioned on Trimouille Island, closer to the explosion. Here, there were a plethora of blast, pressure and seismographic gauges. There were also some 200 empty petrol tins for measuring the blast, a technique that Penney had employed on Operation Crossroads. There were thermometers and calorimeters for measuring the flash, and samples of paints and fabrics for determining the effect on them. Plants would be studied to measure their uptake of fission products, particularly radioactive iodine and strontium.

Stores were unloaded at beachhead H2 on Hermite Island, from whence the RAAF had built a road to H1. A stores compound was established at Gladstone Beach on Trimouille Island, known as T3.

The original intention was that the scientists (including my team) would stay on *Campania*, commuting to the islands each day, but the survey party had misjudged the tides; *Campania* could not enter the lagoon and had to anchor in the Parting Pool. The pinnaces could not tie up alongside *Campania* at night and had to be moored several miles away. Transferring to the boats in choppy waters was hazardous.

One scientist fell in the sea and was rescued by Commander Douglas Bromley, *Campania*'s executive officer. Rough seas prevented much work being done between 10 and 14 August. It took about an hour and a half to get from *Campania* to H2, and travelling between *Plym* and *Campania* took between two and three hours. Even when a boat was on call it could take 45 minutes to respond. Boat availability soon became a problem with only five LCMs, leaving personnel waiting for one to arrive.

The twelve smaller LCAs were also employed; although they could operate when the tides made waters too shallow for the pinnaces, their wooden bottoms were easily holed by coral outcrops. On 15 August, some men were transferred from *Campania* by one of its three Dragonfly helicopters, but the weather closed in and they could not be picked up again, having to find shelter on *Tracker* and *Zeebrugge*, which were moored in the lagoon.

To get around these problems, tented camps were established for the scientists at H1 on Hermite Island and Cocoa Beach (also known as T2) on Trimouille Island. My team was split into the two camps.

Scientific rehearsals were held on 12 and 13 September. This was followed by an operational rehearsal on 19 September, which included fully assembling the bomb, since the radioactive components had arrived the day before on a Sunderland.

Penney arrived by air on 22 September. Everything was in readiness by 30 September, and the only remaining factor was the weather. This was unfavourable on 1 October but improved the following day, when Penney designated 3 October as the date for the test. The final countdown commenced at 09:15 local time on 3 October 1952.

The bomb was successfully detonated at 09:29:24 on 3 October 1952 local time, which was 23:59:24 on 2 October 1952 UTC, 00:59:24 on 3 October in London, and 7:59:24 on 3 October in Perth. The explosion occurred 8 feet 10 inches (2.7 m) below the water line and left a saucer-shaped crater on the seabed 20 feet (6 m) deep and 980 feet (300 m) across.

The yield was estimated at 25 kilotons of TNT (100 TJ). All that was left of *Plym* was a "gluey black substance" that washed up on the shore of Trimouille Island. The bomb had performed exactly as expected.

Two Dragonfly helicopters flew in to gather a sample of contaminated seawater from the lagoon. Scientists in gas masks and protective gear visited various points in pinnaces to collect samples and retrieve recordings. Tracker controlled this aspect, as it had the decontamination facilities. Air samples were collected by RAAF Avro Lincoln aircraft. Although the feared tidal surge had not occurred, radioactive contamination of the islands was widespread and severe.

It was clear that had an atomic bomb exploded in a British port, it would have been a catastrophe worse than the bombing of Hiroshima and Nagasaki. The fallout cloud rose to 10,000 feet (3,000 m) and was blown out to sea, as intended, but later reversed direction and blew over the Australian mainland. Very low levels of radioactivity were detected as far away as Brisbane.

Penney and some of his staff returned by air on 9 October. He was appointed a Knight Commander of the British Empire on 23 October 1952 for his role in Operation Hurricane. Torlesse was supposed to accompany him, but in view of the degree of radioactive contamination, he felt he could not leave his command. He sent Captain D. P. Willan, the skipper of Narvik in his stead. The Royal Navy ships departed the Montebello Islands on 31 October. Most of the scientific staff were dropped off at Fremantle and returned to Britain on RAF Transport Command aircraft. The rest returned on Campania, which arrived in the United Kingdom on 15 December. Hawkesbury continued to patrol the area until 15 January 1953.

My team returned with their documentation by RAF Transport. Our task had now begun: transferring the files of the personnel, and the test results; the number of documents that had been written during the preparation and execution of the tests was extraordinary. All personnel had a file which was updated with duties, exposure levels and their time spent doing each duty. Their proximity to the explosion was also recorded and for some, it was too close.

With the success of Operation Hurricane, Britain became the third nuclear power after the United States and the Soviet Union. Four weeks after Operation Hurricane, the United States successfully demonstrated a hydrogen bomb. The technology mastered in Operation Hurricane was six years old, and with the hydrogen bomb in hand, the US Congress saw no benefit in renewing cooperation. All the while Britain strove for independence, at the same time it sought interdependence in the form of a renewal of the Special Relationship with the United States. As successful as it was, Operation Hurricane fell short on both counts.

The Montebello Islands and the surrounding area were damaged forever; the effect on the area was devastating and beyond what any theory had imagined. The documentary evidence proved that the fallout had exceeded the simulations and, because of changing wind patterns, the fallout could not be controlled.

We continued to receive updates from the Hawkesbury and the personnel on board. Tests carried out by the personnel proved that the contamination was far greater than first thought.

To compete with the Americans, Britain needed to continue its tests and develop a hydrogen bomb of its own.

# Chapter 10 – Blue Danube

Our work continued. Monitoring reports started to be delivered to my team from various sources across the world. Doctors reported on radiation poisoning: the illnesses of the armed forces personnel were monitored and those in the NP ranges 1-5 were found to have significant issues, ranging from sickness to skin conditions.

I was called to a meeting to discuss the way forward for the British nuclear testing programme. The British government needed to develop an H bomb, which could be delivered by an RAF V bomber. The scientists continued to work on the technology and another test site was being discussed, this time in Maralinga, which is in the remote western area of South Australia.

Blue Danube was the first operational British nuclear weapon. It also went by a variety of other names, including Smallboy, the Mk.1 Atom Bomb, Special Bomb and OR.1001, a reference to the operational requirement it was built to fill.

The RAF V bomber force was initially meant to use Blue Danube as their primary armament at a time when the first hydrogen bomb had not been detonated, and the British military planners still believed that an atomic war could be fought and won using atomic bombs of similar yield to the Hiroshima bomb. For that reason, the stockpile planned was for up to 800 bombs with yields of 10-12 kilotons. When their plans were formulated, V bomber bomb bays were sized to carry Blue Danube, the smallest-size nuclear bomb that was possible to be designed given the technology of the day.

These planning meetings were long affairs, with scientists and military personnel often at loggerheads about the design and implementation of this device.

Blue Danube added a ballistic-shaped casing to the existing Hurricane physics package, with four flip-out fins to ensure a stable ballistic trajectory from the planned release height of 50,000 ft. It initially used a plutonium core, but all service versions were modified to use a composite plutonium/U-235 core, and a version was also tested with a uranium-only core. The service chiefs insisted on a yield of between 10-12 kt for two reasons: firstly, to minimise usage of scarce and expensive fissile material; and secondly, to minimise the risk of predetonation, a phenomenon then little understood, and the primary reason for using a composite core of concentric shells of plutonium and U-235. Although there were many plans for versions with higher yields, some up to 40 kt, none were developed, largely because of the scarcity of fissile materials, and there is no evidence that any were seriously contemplated.

The first Blue Danube was delivered to stockpile at RAF Wittering in November 1953 although there were no aircraft equipped to carry it until the following year. No. 1321 Flight RAF was established at RAF Wittering in April 1954 as a Vickers Valiant unit to integrate the Blue Danube nuclear weapon into RAF service. The Short Sperrin was also able to carry the Blue Danube and had been ordered as a fall-back option, in case the V bomber projects proved unsuccessful. Declassified archives show that 58 were produced before production shifted in 1958 to the smaller and more capable Red Beard weapon, which could accept the Blue Danube fissile core and be carried by much smaller aircraft. It seems unlikely that all 58 Blue Danube weapons were operational at any given time. Blue Danube was retired in 1962.

Bomb storage facilities for the weapon were built at RAF Barnham in Suffolk and RAF Faldingworth in Lincolnshire. These sites were built specifically to store bomb components in small buildings called 'hutches', with the high explosive elements of the weapons stored in dedicated storage areas. The storage facilities were closed in 1963 and put up for sale in 1966, the Barnham site becoming an industrial estate. The site at Barnham is a scheduled monument.

Major deficiencies with Blue Danube included the use of unreliable lead-acid accumulators to supply power to the firing circuits and radar altimeters. Later weapons used the more reliable ram-air turbine-generators or thermal batteries. Blue Danube was not engineered as a weapon equipped to withstand the rigours of service life; it was a scientific experiment on a gigantic scale, which needed to be re-engineered to meet service requirements, resulting in Red Beard. The same could be said of the first US atomic bomb, Fat Man, which was quickly re-engineered after World War II.

My team now had more personnel to monitor, at locations across the globe, with personnel split into many sections also stationed around the world. The storage of the weapons was meticulously recorded, with each person exposed to the weapon becoming a subject of the NMC.

To cope with demand, I requested more personnel be enlisted into my team. We already had a backlog of information processing and due to the manual process of classifying, storing and filing of information (you have to remember that we did not have computers, databases or clever software packages), my request was granted, and my team doubled.

# Chapter 11 – Emu Field: The Tests

Emu Field is in the desert of South Australia. Variously known as Emu Field, Emu Junction or Emu, it was chosen over Maralinga as the next testing site due to its remote location. The operation was codenamed Totem and would consist of a pair of nuclear tests, scheduled for 15 October 1953.

The main purpose of the Totem trial was to determine the acceptable limit on the amount of plutonium-240 which could be present in a bomb. The plutonium used in the original Hurricane device was produced in a nuclear reactor at Windscale. This plant did not have anything like the capacity to provide enough material for the British government's planned weapons programme, and consequently eight more reactors had been planned.

These were intended to produce both electricity and plutonium, and the design was known as Pippa, (for Pressurised Pile Producing Power and Plutonium). Construction of the first one started at Calder Hall in March 1953. However, for cost reasons they were to operate in such a way that a higher proportion of plutonium-240 was to be present in the fissionable plutonium-239 product than in the Windscale-produced material. This was potentially a problem since plutonium-240 is prone to spontaneous fission, which would both present a criticality accident risk and reduce the likely yield of any weapon containing it. Sir William Penney urgently obtained ministerial permission in December 1952, two months after the Hurricane shot, for the Totem tests to take place in October 1953.

The Totem tests tried two designs with different proportions of plutonium-240 in the pit. Since the Royal Navy were unable to provide the level of support which they had in the Hurricane test, the Montebello Islands used for that shot were ruled out. Instead a new site, originally given the codename X200 but later renamed Emu Field, was selected following surveys by Len Beadell and the British Army Survey Corps. An isolated dry, flat clay and sandstone expanse in the Great Victoria Desert, it was 480 km north west of Woomera, South

Australia.

Because the site was on the Australian mainland, the Australian government required much more information than they had for the Hurricane test, including details of the implosion principle behind the bomb's design and much more information about nuclear fallout and radioactive contamination. The isolated location and poor roads meant that only 500 tons of the 3,000 tons of equipment needed for the test arrived by road, the bulk arriving via the airstrip and quickly constructed on the site (about 17 kilometres north west of the test field on a lake bed). The main scientific party arrived on 17 August and the device for the first test arrived on 26 September, to be followed three days later by Penney.

My team was again tasked with logging all personnel present at these tests and specifically looking at any personnel present at both Operations Hurricane and Totem. Personnel who were present at both tests were given a new NP rating, with a number added to the beginning of their rating.

So, for any person present at one operation, a 1 was inserted, so NP1 became 1NP1. If they were present at another operation, it was changed to a 2, so it became 2NP1. Their NP rating was also assessed on both operations, so if they were NP10 at the first operation, it would remain 1NP10, but the second operation could be a different rating, 2NP5, for instance.

My team was sent to the area to again document the experiment, and the personnel involved, and this time I was asked to attend the test. As well as the main tests, a series of smaller tests would also be carried out and each needed careful monitoring reports created.

The two nuclear explosions were preceded by five smaller tests which formed part of a series codenamed Kittens, and which were performed without formal Australian government approval. These did not produce nuclear explosions, but used conventional explosive and polonium-210, beryllium and natural uranium to investigate the performance of neutron initiators.

*Totem 1* was detonated on 15 October 1953 and *Totem 2* was detonated on 27 October 1953. The devices were both sited on towers and yielded 9 kilotons and 7 kilotons respectively.

Efforts were made to prevent nomadic Aboriginal people from entering the area around the test site, but there were thought to be no (or at most very few) people in such a dry and inhospitable environment. The chief scientist at the Australian Department of Supply, W. A. S. Butement asserted that "I am given to understand that the area is no longer used by Aborigines". The precautions consisted of warnings sent to pastoral stations in August 1953, warning notices around the perimeter of the test site, and aerial and ground searches, usually within 20 miles of the site, which were made with increasing frequency as the test firings approached. The 1985 Royal Commission into British nuclear tests in Australia determined that the area was still being occasionally used and the efforts have been criticised as inadequate.

Before the tests, the height of the radioactive cloud resulting from the explosions was estimated at 12,000 feet, (+/-1000 feet). This led to safety criteria for making the decision to detonate the device that the wind direction from ground level up to 10,000 feet should not lie between 330 and 130 degrees and that no rain was forecast closer than 200 miles downwind. However, the cloud from the *Totem 1* shot rose to 15,000 feet, drifting east and crossing the coast 50 hours later near Townsville.

Following the *Totem 1* test, a black mist rolled across the landscape at the Wallatina and Welbourn Hill stations in the Granite Downs 175 km from the test site and led to unacceptably high levels of radioactive contamination of these locations. There is controversy surrounding injuries received by Aboriginal people from fallout, and from this mist. Approximately 45 Yankunytjatjara people were reported to have been caught in the mist at Wallatina and fallen ill, and over half may have died.

The 1985 Royal Commission concluded that "Aboriginal people experienced radioactive fallout from *Totem 1* in the form of a black mist or cloud at or near Wallatina. This may have made some people temporarily ill. The Royal Commission does not have sufficient evidence to say whether or not it caused other illnesses or injuries".

The *Totem 2* cloud rose even higher, to 28,000 feet because of condensation of moisture entrained in it, and whilst the wind direction below 12,000 feet was an acceptable 10 degrees, at 20,000 feet it was 270 degrees. However, high winds dispersed the cloud so that it had dissipated to the point where it could not be tracked beyond around 310 miles east of the test site.

I was watching from 25 miles away. To witness such an explosion in real life – not just through reading reports – was the most frightening experience I have ever encountered. The sheer power of this man-made device and the destruction, not only at the time but for years to come, was unbelievable and the fact that the British government was prepared to detonate such a weapon, on mainland close to civilians, still makes me shudder. I was only monitoring the armed forces personnel; no one monitored the civilian population.

A few days after these tests and what I thought was the end of the testing in this area, I was summoned to a meeting as the British government had formally requested a permanent testing site from the Australian government, which led to an agreement on the use of the Maralinga test site in August 1954. But before this, a further Operation codenamed Mosaic was to use the already decimated Montebello Islands.

I was asked to monitor a different aspect following the Totem tests. An unmanned British Centurion tank, Registration Number 169041, was positioned around 500 yards (460 m) from ground zero at the *Totem I* test. Following the test the tank's light damage was repaired and it was put back into service. We instigated a monitoring procedure of the tank, and any personnel who encountered it were also monitored.

169041, subsequently nicknamed *The Atomic Tank*, was later used in the Vietnam War. In May 1969, during a firefight, 169041 (call sign 24C) was hit by a rocket-propelled grenade (RPG) but remained battleworthy.

*The Atomic Tank* is now located at Robertson Barracks in Palmerston, Northern Territory. Although other tanks were subjected to nuclear tests, 169041 is the only tank known to have withstood atomic tests and subsequently gone on for another 23 years of service, including 15 months on operational deployment in a war zone.

We were preparing more and more documents; the indexing system was increasing in complexity and the volumes of files were becoming unmanageable. I questioned my superiors and asked if these latest tests would be the end of the personnel monitoring and that no further tests would be carried out. I was told that more tests would follow, that they would increase in size and destruction, and that the number of personnel would increase.

# Chapter 12 – Operation Mosaic

I was flown to Aldermaston for the planning of Operation Mosaic. I now had over 100 people in my department, spread across the world, and the management of the monitoring was becoming a major undertaking.

I agreed to stay and for my efforts, I was awarded an MBE for services to the government. Whilst I was proud to receive such an award, it was tainted as I was starting to see the after effects of the testing programme.

Like Operation Hurricane before it, Mosaic was a Royal Navy responsibility. Planning commenced in February 1955 under the codename Operation Giraffe. In June 1955, the Admiralty adopted the codename Operation Mosaic. The Atomic Trials Executive in London, chaired by Lieutenant General Sir Frederick Morgan, had already begun planning Operation Buffalo. It assumed responsibility for Operation Mosaic as well, sitting as Mosex or Buffalex as appropriate. Captain Hugh Martell would be in charge as commander of Task Force 308, with the temporary rank of commodore. Charles Adams from Aldermaston, who had been the deputy technical director to Leonard Tyte for Operation Hurricane and to William Penney on Operation Totem, was appointed the scientific director for Operation Mosaic, with Ieuan Maddock as the scientific superintendent. Group Captain S.W.B. (Paddy) Menaul would command the Air Task Group. Menaul was also a nuclear test veteran, having been an observer on board Vickers Valiant WZ366 when it had made the first operational drop of a British atomic bomb during Operation Totem. Planning was conducted at Aldermaston.

These planning meetings were long and complicated affairs, with senior officials and civil servants often at loggerheads over the planning and execution.

On 18 July 1955 a five-man mission headed by Martell that included Adams, Menaul and Lieutenant Commanders A. K. Dodds and R. R. Fotheringham departed the UK for Australia. They arrived on 22

July and began a series of discussions. The Australian government created a Montebello Working Party as a subcommittee of the Maralinga Committee as a counterpart to the British Mosex. Adams met with W.A.S. Butement of the recently-formed Atomic Weapons Tests Safety Committee (AWTSC) and agreed at least two of its members would be present on board the Task Force 308 flagship, the Landing Ship, Tank, HMS *Narvik*, when the decision to fire was taken. He also had discussions with Leonard Dwyer, the director of the Australian Bureau of Meteorology, about the weather conditions that could be expected for the test. It was agreed that a Royal Australian Navy (RAN) frigate would act as a weather ship for the test series, and that a second weather ship might be required to give warnings of cyclones.

As a founder member of the AWTSC and still head of the NMC, I was asked to be present on the flagship. Having seen the destruction caused by Totem, I declined and one of my senior officials was sent instead. This decision was one made for self-preservation and was selfish. My senior official was subsequently diagnosed with cancer and died aged 47. I do not know if this was due to his exposure, but I do know he was classed as an NP2 when he was monitored by the department and he was fit and healthy before he attended the tests. He left a wife and a young son. I had no family and could easily have gone in his place. This guilt I will take to my grave.

A small fleet of ships was assembled for Operation Mosaic. HMS *Narvik* began a refit at HM Dockyard, Chatham, in July 1955, and was completed by November. She departed the UK on 29 December 1955, and travelled via the Suez Canal, reaching Fremantle on 23 February 1956. The frigate HMS *Alert*, normally the yacht of the Commander-in-Chief, Far East Fleet, was loaned to act as an accommodation ship for scientists and VIPs. Along with the tanker RFA *Eddyrock*, they formed Task Group 308.1. The Far East Fleet also supplied the cruiser HMS *Newfoundland*, and destroyers HMS *Cossack*, *Concord*, *Consort* and *Comus*. These formed Task Group 308.3. The destroyer HMS *Diana* was detailed to carry out scientific tests and formed Task Group 308.4.

They were augmented by RAN vessels, designated Task Group 308.2. The sloop HMAS *Warrego* and boom defence vessel *Karangi* carried out a hydrographic survey of the Montebello Islands, laying marker buoys for moorings. Care had to be taken with this, as Operation Hurricane had left some parts of the islands dangerously radioactive.

The corvettes HMAS *Fremantle* and HMAS *Junee* provided logistical support, ferried personnel between the islands and the mainland, and accommodated 14 Australian and British media representatives during the first test. They were replaced by *Karangi* for the second test. A pair of RANS 120ft motor lighters, MWL251 and MRL252, provided water and refrigeration respectively. The two barges were visited by the First Sea Lord, Admiral Lord Mountbatten, and Lady Mountbatten, who flew out to the islands on a Whirlwind helicopter on 15 April.

Only a small party of Royal Engineers and two Aldermaston scientists travelled on *Narvik*. The main scientific party left London by air on 1 April. The Air Task Group consisted of 107 officers and 407 other ranks. Most were based at Pearce and Onslow, although four RAF Shackletons and about 70 RAF personnel were based at Darwin, from whence the Shackletons daily flew weather reconnaissance flights, commencing on 2 March. There was a cyclone three days later. Three Royal Australian Air Force (RAAF) Neptunes flew safety patrols, five RAF Varsity aircraft tracked clouds and flew on low-level radiological survey missions, five RAF Canberra bombers were tasked with collecting radioactive samples, four RAF Hastings aircraft flew between the UK and Australia, and two Whirlwind helicopters provided a taxi service. The United States Air Force (USAF) provided a pair of C-118 Liftmasters to collect radioactive samples. Lieutenant-Colonel R. N. B. Holmes was in charge of the Royal Engineers, whose tasks including erecting the 300-foot (91 m) aluminium towers for the shots.

We now had departments in Australia, America and the UK, and the monitoring programme had taken on hundreds of personnel. We had representatives in each government, with the NP tags applied to records across the world.

Adams arrived at Montebello on 22 April and was sufficiently impressed with the progress of works to schedule a scientific rehearsal for 27 April. A second scientific rehearsal was held on 2 May, followed by a full dress rehearsal on 5 May. The fissile material was delivered by an RAF Hastings to Onslow, collected by HMS *Alert* on 11 May and delivered to the Montebello Islands the following day. Five members of the AWTSC – Leslie H. Martin, Ernest Titterton, Cecil Eddy, Butement and Dwyer – arrived at Onslow and were flown to *Narvik* by helicopter on 14 May. The following day, Martell set 16 May as the day for the test. There had been protests in Perth at the test series, and the Deputy Premier of Western Australia, John Tonkin, promised to discuss demands for an end to the tests. Martin and Titterton confronted Martell and Adams, and Martin told them that without enough information about the nature of the tests, the AWTSC could not approve them. That it had a veto came as a surprise; it was not what their orders from London said. Penney sent a message to Adams on 10 May:

*"Strongly advise not showing Safety Committee any significant weapon details but would not object to their seeing outside of cabled ball in centre section. They could be told that fissile material is at centre of large ball of high explosive and that elaborate electronics necessary to get symmetrical squash. No details of explosives configuration or inner components must be revealed. Appreciate that the position is awkward for you and that you must make minor concessions."*

Rather than stonewall, Adams and Martell disclosed the same information that had been given to Menzies, on condition that they kept it to themselves. This mollified them, and the G1 test went ahead. The device was detonated on Trimouille Island at 03:50 UTC (11:50 local time) on 16 May. Soon afterwards, *Narvik* and *Alert* entered the Parting Pool. The Radiological Group, wearing full protective clothing, entered the lagoon in a cutter. They retrieved measuring instruments and conducted a ground survey. A tent with a decontamination area was established ashore, and a water pump allowed the Radiological Group to wash themselves before they returned to *Narvik*.

The main danger to the ships' crews was from radioactive seaweed, so the crews were prohibited from catching or eating fish, and ships' evaporators were not run. Spot checks were made to verify that there was no contamination on board. Most of the sample collection was completed by 20 May. An extra run was made to collect film badges from Hermite Island, and Maddock paid the crater a visit on 25 May to collect further samples. Two RAF Canberra bombers – one of which was flown by Menaul – flew through the cloud to collect samples.

The film badges were collected and stored with the personnel records to ascertain any levels of radiation exposure.

The results of the test were mixed. The yield was between 15 and 20 kilotonnes of TNT (63 and 84 TJ), as had been anticipated, although the mushroom cloud rose to 21,000 feet (6,400 m) instead of 14,000 feet (4,300 m) as predicted. Valuable data was obtained. The implosion system had performed flawlessly, but the boosting effect of the lithium deuteride had been negligible; the boosting process had not been fully understood. Given the result of G1, plans were changed for G2. It had been intended to use a lead tamper for G2, but given the low yield of G1, a natural uranium tamper was substituted. HMS *Diana*, about 6 miles (9.7 km) from ground zero, was quickly decontaminated, and sailed for Singapore on 18 May. The fallout cloud initially moved out to sea as predicted, but then reversed direction and drifted across northern Australia. Tests on the aircraft at Onslow had detected signs of radioactive contamination from G1, indicating that some fallout had been blown over the mainland.

These findings of contamination were sealed in a specially designed container within our monitoring vault. I was not allowed access to these findings and to my knowledge, they are still sealed, or may have been destroyed, as the findings could lead to major compensation claims due because of the fallout across the mainland.

Scientific rehearsals for G2 were held on 28 and 31 May, followed by a full rehearsal on 4 June. The fissile core for the device was delivered to Onslow by RAF Hastings on 6 June, and once again couriered to the Montebello Islands by HMS *Alert*. There then followed a period of waiting for suitable weather conditions. These were not common at this time of the year; at the start of Operation Mosaic, it had been estimated that conditions favourable for G2 would occur only three days per month. In fact, since *Narvik* had arrived in March, not a single day had been suitable. And good weather conditions alone were insufficient; the meteorologists had to accurately forecast them. As the 15 July deadline drew nearer, William Cook, the scientist in charge of the hydrogen bomb project at Aldermaston, determined that in view of the results of G1, G2 was now more important than ever.

Another complication was safety. While the test of a larger device would normally mandate a larger safety area, Beale announced that G2 was going to be smaller than G1. To avoid embarrassing the minister, the safety area was not enlarged, and no official announcement was made that G2 would in fact be larger. The weather improved on 8 June, and Martell ordered the countdown to begin the following day, but Beale objected to a test being carried out on a Sunday. During Operation Totem there was an agreement that no tests would be conducted on Sundays. Mosex considered that matter in London and directed Martell not to test. The following 48 hours were unsuitable. On 17 June the meteorologists predicted a break in the weather and Martell ordered the countdown to recommence.

G2 was detonated from a tower on Alpha Island at 02:14 UTC (10:14 local time) on 19 June. It produced a yield of 60 kilotonnes of TNT (250 TJ), making it the largest nuclear device ever detonated in Australia.

The cloud rose to 47,000 feet (14,000 m), considerably higher than the predicted 37,000 feet (11,000 m). The procedure for collecting samples was far more limited than that of G1. A land rover was landed from a Landing Craft Assault (LCA) and driven by a party wearing protective clothing to within 400 feet (120 m) of ground zero to collect samples and recover the blast measurement equipment.

As these personnel had been the closest to a detonation site, our coding system no longer functioned correctly. NP1 could no longer be classified as the highest exposure and we needed to insert an additional indicator for these personnel. We decided on an asterisk so NP1 became NP1* and these were flagged as the personnel with the highest exposure possibility.

Another sortie was made to collect film badges from Hermite Island, and Maddock collected a sample from the G2 crater. The Canberra sent to fly through the cloud had trouble finding it, and only after some searching located it about 80 miles (130 km) from where it was supposed to be. The following day, the Canberra sent to track the cloud and collect more samples could not locate it at all. The bulk of the fallout drifted over the Arafura Sea, but owing to different winds at different altitudes, part of it again drifted over the mainland.

As fallout was detected over northern Australia by monitoring stations, in combination with Beale's announcement that G2 would be smaller than G1, an impression was generated that something had gone horribly wrong. The acting Prime Minister, Sir Arthur Fadden, ordered an inquiry. Seamen in Fremantle demanded that the SS *Koolinda*, a cattle transport on which 75 cattle had died, be inspected, as it was feared that they had died from radioactive poisoning. The seamen refused to unload the remaining 479 cattle. A physicist from the Commonwealth X-Ray and Radium Laboratory (CXRL) with a Geiger counter found no evidence of radioactive contamination, and the deaths were determined to have resulted from red water disease. It was estimated that someone living in Port Hedland, where the contamination was highest, would receive a dose of 580 microsieverts (0.058 rem) over a period of 50 years, if they wore no clothes.

The results of the Geiger counter did find radioactive contamination, but the results were never disclosed. The report was logged and discussed at a meeting at which I was present; it was decided not to disclose the information but blame the issue on red water disease. This was the first time that I had experienced the lies and deceit that would form the basis of my work over the next 50 years.

By the 1980s, the radioactivity had decayed to the point where it was no longer hazardous to the casual visitor, but there were still radioactive metal fragments. The island remained a prohibited area until 1992. A 2006 zoological survey found that the wildlife had recovered. As part of the Gorgon gas project, rats and feral cats were eradicated from the Montebello Islands in 2009, and birds and marsupials were transplanted from nearby Barrow Island to Hermite Island. Today, the Montebello Islands are a park. Visitors are advised not to spend more than an hour per day at the test sites, or to take relics of the tests as souvenirs. A pyramid-shaped obelisk marks the site of the G2 explosion on Alpha Island.

We now had amassed thousands of documents, with evidence of radioactive fallout to civilian populations, the contamination of the earth, the devastation to the eco system and the start of evidence of the damage it was doing to the personnel involved.

# Chapter 13 – Operation Buffalo

As Emu Field was now considered to be too remote and had been contaminated by Operation Mosaic, I attended another meeting to discuss a further test, codenamed Operation Buffalo.

Maralinga was part of the Woomera Prohibited Area in South Australia and lies about 500 miles (800 km) north-west of Adelaide. A local tribe (Maralinga Tjarutja) inhabited the area, but it was still chosen to perform trials and two major tests.

Operation Buffalo commenced on 27 September 1956. The operation consisted of the testing of four nuclear devices, codenamed *One Tree*, *Marcoo*, *Kite* and *Breakaway* respectively. *One Tree* (12.9 kilotonnes of TNT (54 TJ)) and *Breakaway* (10.8 kilotonnes of TNT (45 TJ)) were exploded from towers, *Marcoo* (1.4 kilotonnes of TNT (5.9 TJ)) was exploded at ground level, and *Kite* (2.9 kilotonnes of TNT (12 TJ)) was released by a Royal Air Force Vickers Valiant bomber from a height of 35,000 feet (11,000 m). This was the first drop of a British nuclear weapon from an aircraft.

The fallout from these tests was measured using sticky paper, air sampling devices, and water sampled from rainfall and reservoirs. The radioactive cloud from *Buffalo 1 (One Tree)* reached a height of 37,500 ft (11,400 m), exceeding the predicted 27,900 ft (8,500 m), and radioactivity was detected in South Australia, Northern Territory, New South Wales, and Queensland. All four Buffalo tests were criticised by the 1985 McClelland Royal Commission, which concluded that they were fired under inappropriate conditions.

In 2001, Dr Sue Rabbit Roff, a researcher from the University of Dundee, uncovered documentary evidence that troops had been ordered to run, walk and crawl across areas contaminated by the Buffalo tests in the days immediately following the detonations; a fact that the British government later admitted. Dr Roff stated that "it puts the lie to the British government's claim that they never used humans for guinea pig-type experiments in nuclear weapons trials in Australia."

I can confirm her evidence. She uncovered one document; the

British government has access to thousands which confirm that the personnel involved were experimented on. We were and still are monitoring their lives across the world.

Operation Buffalo involved more personnel, some of whom again were present at some of the previous tests. We now had one person in our archives who was classified as a 3NP1*, which meant that he had been at three operations and exposed to the highest level of contamination.

We needed to monitor these personnel more closely. We introduced a grading system and the top five per cent of the personnel were placed on the 'At-Risk' register, which meant we believed that they or their families would soon start to see the effects of the tests on their bodies and through their children.

# Chapter 14 – Operation Antler

Operation Antler followed in 1957. Antler was designed to test components for thermonuclear weapons, with emphasis on triggering mechanisms. Three tests began in September, codenamed *Tadje*, *Biak* and *Taranaki*. The first two tests were conducted from towers; the last was suspended from balloons. Yields from the weapons were 0.93 kilotonnes of TNT (3.9 TJ), 5.67 kilotonnes of TNT (23.7 TJ) and 26.6 kilotonnes of TNT (111 TJ) respectively.

The *Tadje* test used cobalt pellets as a 'tracer' for determining yield; later, rumours developed that Britain had been developing a cobalt bomb. The Royal Commission found that personnel handling these pellets were later exposed to the active cobalt-60. Although the Antler series was better planned and organised than earlier series, intermediate fallout from the Taranaki test exceeded predictions.

To put this into perspective, cobalt-60 is a synthetic radioactive isotope of cobalt with a half-life of 5.2714 years. It is produced artificially in nuclear reactors.

We now had another problem with our coding system. For those people who had been exposed to cobalt, we needed to classify them differently, so a C was added to the exposure grading and a scale of 1-10 added, so a person could now become 1NP1C1, which would state that they were at one operation, exposed to the highest level and exposed to cobalt at the highest level.

Anyone who was exposed to cobalt was immediately put into the top five per cent of our test subjects due to the risk of contracting cancer.

In addition to the major tests, many minor trials were also carried out from June 1955 and extended through to April 1963. Although the major tests had been exposed to some publicity, the minor tests were carried out in absolute secrecy. These minor tests left a dangerous legacy of radioactive contamination at Maralinga.

The four series of minor trials were codenamed Kittens, Tims, Rats and Vixen. In all, these trials included up to 700 tests, some involving experiments with plutonium, uranium, and beryllium. Operation Kittens involved 99 trials, performed at both Maralinga and Emu Field in 1953-1961. The tests were used in the development of neutron initiators, involving use of polonium-210 and uranium, and generated "relatively large amounts of radioactive contamination". Operation Tims took place in 1955-1963, and involved 321 trials of uranium and beryllium tampers, as well as studies of plutonium compression. Operation Rats investigated explosive dispersal of uranium. One hundred and twenty-five trials took place between 1956 and 1960.

The Vixen minor trials (Vixen A and Vixen B) were formulated to investigate what would happen to a nuclear device which burnt or was subject to a non-nuclear explosion. Thirty-one Vixen A trials between 1959 and 1961 investigated the effects of an accidental fire on a nuclear weapon and involved a total of about 1 kg of plutonium. Twelve Vixen B trials, between 1960 and 1963, attempted to discover the effects of high explosives detonating a nuclear weapon in a fire (typical of conditions which would occur in aviation accidents) and involved 22 kg of plutonium. They produced "jets of molten, burning plutonium extending hundreds of feet into the air". It was the lack of subsequent disposal of the plutonium from these minor trials – Vixen B especially – which created the major radiation problems at the site.

The Vixen experimental tests used TNT to blow up simulated nuclear warheads containing plutonium-239. In total, Vixen B scattered 22.2 kg of plutonium around the Maralinga test site known as Taranaki, in particles of widely divergent size. Plutonium is not particularly dangerous externally – it emits alpha particles which are stopped by 9 cm (3.5 in) of air, or the dead layer of skin cells on the body, and is not a very intensive source of radiation, due to its long half-life of 24,000 years. It is most dangerous when it enters the body, in the worst case by breathing, and therefore tiny particles, often the result of such explosion testing, are the worst threat. The extreme biological persistence of plutonium's radioactive contamination and the cancer threat posed by alpha radiation occurring internally together establish plutonium's dangers.

In terms of regular nuclear testing, Kittens represents bomb component testing, while Tims and Rats were early subcritical hydro nuclear tests. Vixen is 'safety testing' of a bomb; assuring that the core would not accidentally undergo criticality in the event of a fire or unintended crash. These are always messy (see the US equivalent at Plutonium Valley in Project 56), for a successful test subjects the core fuel to high explosives in the hope that it simply scatters rather than undergoes criticality. The differences in the sort of dangers presented by the major versus minor tests is that there was no critical explosion in the minor tests. In the major tests, the bomb cores reached critical mass; the plutonium or uranium fissile materials "burned" into highly radioactive fission products, and those, along with the unspent fuel and activated bomb case, tower and soil if the explosion was close to the ground, are lofted into the stratosphere to be dropped eventually as fallout globally. In Vixen, an equivalent amount of plutonium fuel was simply smashed by explosives and spread about much more locally. In Kittens, Tims and Rats, smaller amounts of various materials were similar exploded locally and spread about.

Following the tests, the highest level of classification was stamped onto the documentation produced at Maralinga. The contamination levels were so high that the British government would go to any lengths to protect the documentation.

It was during the transfer of the documents to microfiche for easier storage that nuclear veteran Avon Hudson became a whistle-blower and spoke out to the media in the 1970s. His disclosures helped pave the way towards a public inquiry into the tests and their legacy.

The McClelland Royal Commission of 1984-1985 identified significant residual contamination at some sites. British and Australian servicemen were purposely exposed to fallout from the blasts, to study radiological effects. The local Aboriginal people have claimed they were poisoned by the tests and, in 1994, the Australian government reached a compensation settlement with Maralinga Tjarutja of $13.5 million in settlement of all claims in relation to the nuclear testing.

If the Tjarutja had known the extent of the contamination, they would not have settled for $13.5 million. The contamination levels are extremely high in Maralinga.

In January 1985, the Maralinga Tjarutja native title land was handed over to the Maralinga people under the Maralinga Tjarutja Land Rights Act, 1984 passed by both houses of the South Australian Parliament in December 1984 and proclaimed in January 1987.

In 2003, South Australian Premier Mike Rann and Education Minister Trish White opened a new school at Oak Valley, replacing what had been described as the "worst school in Australia".[2] In May 2004, following the passage of special legislation, Premier Rann handed back title to over 8,000 square miles (21,000 sq km) of land to the Maralinga Tjarutja and Pila Nguru people.

The land, 620 miles (1000 km) northwest of Adelaide and abutting the Western Australia border, was called the Unnamed Conservation Park. It is now known as Mamungari Conservation Park. It includes the Serpentine Lakes and was the largest land return since Premier John Bannon's hand over of Maralinga lands in 1984. At the 2004 ceremony Premier Rann said the return of the land fulfilled a promise he made in 1991 when he was Aboriginal Affairs Minister, after he passed legislation to return lands including the sacred Ooldea area (which also included the site of Daisy Bates' mission camp) to the Maralinga Tjarutja people.

Under an agreement between the governments of the United Kingdom and Australia, efforts were made to clean up the site before the Maralinga people resettled on the land in 1995. They named their new community Oak Valley: it is approximately 80 miles (128 km) NNW of the original township. The effectiveness of the clean-up has been disputed on several occasions.

The population is generally around 23-50. During special cultural activities with visitors from neighbouring communities, it rises to 1,500 people.

*Maralinga: Australia's Nuclear Waste Cover-up* is a book by Alan

---

[2] https://en.wikipedia.org/wiki/Maralinga#cite_note-2

Parkinson about the clean-up of the British atomic bomb test site at Maralinga in South Australia, published in 2007. Parkinson, a nuclear engineer, explains that the clean-up of Maralinga in the late 1990s was compromised by cost-cutting and simply involved dumping hazardous radioactive debris in shallow holes in the ground. Parkinson states that "What was done at Maralinga was a cheap and nasty solution that wouldn't be adopted on white-fellas land."

Whilst this book claims to have evidence of the clean-up and that it was not carried out according to the requirements of a nuclear waste site, he is not far from the truth. The clean-up was compromised, the budget was cut and because of the low numbers of the inhabitants of the area, it was sanctioned by the British government.

The evidence of this is in the NMC archives detailing a report from a nuclear contamination specialist whose findings tell the government not to allow any human being to return to the area, even after the clean-up. This report was ignored, the settlement agreed, and the tribe re-turned. Regular checks performed by the British government have proved that this area is still radioactive, but as it is now the responsibility of the Maralinga Tjarutja, it is no longer their responsibility.

I attended a meeting of the NMC to discuss monitoring the Maralinga Tjarutja tribe. I argued that they should be monitored as part of our programme. If we were to ascertain the levels of contamination at Maralinga, they would be the best subjects. My request was denied, the official response being that we were tasked with monitoring armed forces personnel, not civilians.

These people were taken from their land, which was contaminated and left radioactive. They were returned – and paid for their sacrifice.

Because of the fallout from these operations and the mounting political pressure, the Australian government prohibited hydrogen bomb tests on any Australian soil.

# Chapter 15 – Further Tests

Once Operation Antler had finished, we continued to monitor the personnel from the original testing programme and the effects were starting to filter through our monitoring system.

Personnel were developing cancers at an alarming rate. Suicides were higher than expected, especially amongst those who had higher levels of exposure.

For the personnel who had partners, the level of miscarriage amongst the women was very high. This miscarriage rate was not something that any scientist had expected. DNA was not on the horizon, so we did not understand the human genome.

Why were these women experiencing these issues? Surely it must be through contact with the exposed person?

Further detailed analysis was needed on the women, relating to drugs and medicines available at the time; thalidomide was not yet licensed and had not been prescribed. The contraceptive pill was not yet widely available and there had not yet been any significant breakthroughs in medical science, so why had these miscarriages occurred?

An urgent meeting of the NMC was organised and the findings of our reports were presented to senior military officials and civil servants. I told them that the levels had increased dramatically and there was a connection between the tests and the results.

I was asked, "Can you prove this?" Unfortunately, I could not. All I had were statistics. There was no scientific proof, so it was dismissed as an anomaly.

I was then informed that further nuclear testing was to be carried out under the codename Operation Grapple; it was to be the largest British operation since the D-Day landings. Political pressure was being applied from Russia and the United States – and Britain needed to ensure it was a Nuclear Power.

"But if we expose more personnel and explode more bombs, the scale of the problems we are facing will increase," I replied.

"You will be assigned more personnel to continue your work," was the response.

I left that meeting with a feeling of dread. What was I part of? How had this happened? These personnel had been exposed and no one seemed to care. They were the equivalent of laboratory mice – and I was monitoring them.

Over the next few days, I thought of taking my own life. I could not carry on with this monitoring of human beings. I had a meeting with my senior aide, who informed me that he had cancer and was dying. He had been present at the tests, as I mentioned earlier. I realised I could not give up on him – I had to prove a link between the tests and these horrible diseases and miscarriages. I decided to make it my life's work, documenting evidence and finding the link to help the personnel.

Unfortunately, my senior aide and friend died shortly after of lung cancer; I attribute this to the Maralinga trials at which he was present and his exposure to cobalt-60. He was classified as a 2NP3C1 on his records. How could I have let this happen? I had seen the evidence, I had the records and I let him attend the tests – and now he was dead and his family distraught.

It was at his funeral, when I spoke to his wife, that I decided I would keep copies of documents that I felt relevant to the lies and deceit of the British government. I knew I could be tried for treason and that I would be put in prison or wiped out in a freak accident, but I didn't care anymore. The evidence was such that someone had to stand for the personnel affected.

# Chapter 16 – Operation Grapple

Following my aide's funeral, I took some time off work and holidayed in Tenby, where the coastline is spectacular. Whilst on holiday, I was informed that on my return I was to attend an urgent meeting of the NMC.

I attended the meeting in London at the Cabinet Office; representatives from the United Kingdom Atomic Energy Authority Atomic Weapons Establishment (AWE) at Aldermaston were also present. I was told that, due to the next set of nuclear tests, my department would be expanded and doubled in size for the next three years.

As we could no longer use any Australian controlled island, another test site was required. In the light of the *Lucky Dragon* incident, in which the crew of a Japanese fishing boat were exposed to radioactive fallout from the American Castle Bravo nuclear test, for safety and security reasons a large site remote from population centres was required. Various islands in the South Pacific and Southern Oceans were considered, along with Antarctica. The Admiralty suggested the Antipodes Islands, which are about 530 miles (860 km) south-east of New Zealand. In May 1955, the Minister for Defence, Selwyn Lloyd, concluded that the Kermadec Islands, which lie about 620 miles (1,000 km) north-east of New Zealand, would be suitable.

The islands were part of New Zealand, so Eden wrote to the Prime Minister, Sidney Holland, to ask for permission to use them. Holland refused, fearing an adverse public reaction in the upcoming 1957 general election in his country. Despite reassurances and pressure from the British government, Holland remained firm.

A further meeting was scheduled and the search for a suitable location continued. Malden Island and McKean Island were both considered. These were uninhabited islands claimed by both Britain and the United States. The former island became the frontrunner. Three Avro Shackletons from 240 Squadron were sent to conduct an aerial reconnaissance from Canton Island. It too was claimed by both the United States and Britain, and was jointly administered, so the

Americans had to be informed. Holland agreed to send the survey ship HMNZS *Lachlan* to conduct a maritime survey.

Christmas Island was chosen as a base. It too was claimed by both Britain and the United States. Lying just north of the equator, this tropical island is largely covered in grass, scrub and coconut plantations. Temperatures are high, averaging 88° F (31° C) during the day and 78° F (26° C) at night, and humidity is very high, usually around 98 per cent. Lying 1,450 miles (2,330 km) from Tahiti, 1,335 miles (2,148 km) from Honolulu, 3,250 miles (5,230 km) from San Francisco and 4,000 miles (6,400 km) from Sydney, its remoteness would dominate the logistic preparations for Operation Grapple. It had no indigenous population, but about 260 Gilbertese civilians lived on the island, in a village near Port London. They came from the Gilbert and Ellice Islands, and worked the coconut plantations to produce copra. While most only stayed for a year or two, some had been on the island for a decade or more.

South Pacific Air Lines (SPAL) had been granted permission by the United States and British governments to operate a flying boat service from Christmas Island. Patrick Dean asked the British Ambassador to the United States, Sir Roger Makins to sound out the US government about terminating the contract. Makins reported in March 1956 that Admiral Arthur W. Radford, the Chairman of the Joint Chiefs of Staff, was willing to help so long as the dormant American claim to the island was not prejudiced. The lease on the island facilities, including the airfield and the port, had been granted to SPAL with a clause in the contract that said it could be terminated if there was a military necessity to do so. The Americans proposed that the British tell SPAL they were establishing an airbase on the island, and that the United States would support this so long as SPAL was paid fair compensation. An official letter was sent to the president of SPAL on 1 May 1956, withdrawing the permit to operate from Christmas Island, regretting any inconvenience, and offering to consider compensation.

Rear Admiral Kaye Edden, the Commandant of the Joint Services Staff College, was approached to be the Task Force Commander

(TFC), but he pointed out that the test series would primarily be a Royal Air Force responsibility, and that it would be more appropriate to have an RAF officer in charge. Air Commodore Wilfrid Oulton was appointed Task Force Commander on 6 February 1956, with the acting rank of Air Vice Marshal from 1 March 1956. He secured Group Captain Richard Gething as his Chief of Staff.

At a special meeting of the NMC, I was tasked to be the commander for the monitoring documentation of all personnel. I was promoted and awarded an OBE for my services. I was to liaise directly with Air Commodore Oulton on all matters relating to personnel and the monitoring process.

Group Captain Cecil 'Ginger' Weir was appointed Air Task Group Commander. RAF units assigned to Grapple included two English Electric Canberra bomber squadrons, Nos 76 and 100; two Shackleton squadrons, Nos 206 and 240; the Vickers Valiant bombers of No 49 Squadron; a flight of search and rescue Westland Whirlwind helicopters of No 22 Squadron; and No 1325 Flight with three Dakota transport planes. All would come under the command of No 160 Wing. Cook would be the Scientific Director. Oulton held the first meeting of the Grapple Executive Committee on New Oxford Street in London on 21 February 1956. With pressure mounting at home and abroad for a moratorium on testing, 1 April 1957 was set as the target date.

An advance party arrived on Christmas Island in an RAF Shackleton on 19 June 1956. The Royal Fleet Auxiliary (RFA) *Fort Beauharnois* followed on 23 June and became a temporary headquarters ship. It was ultimately joined by five more RFAs, *Fort Constantine*, *Gold Ranger*, *Fort Rosalie*, *Wave Prince* and *Salvictor*. The role of headquarters ship was assumed by the Landing Ship, Tank (LST) HMS *Messina*, which arrived on 7 December 1956. She was fitted out with special radio equipment to contact the United Kingdom. She carried large refrigerators on her tank deck for storage of fresh and frozen produce and could supply 100 long tons (100 t) of potable water per day.

The light aircraft carrier HMS *Warrior* was the operation control ship, and the flagship of Commodore Peter Gretton, the overall Naval

Task Group commander. She embarked three Grumman TBF Avenger attack aircraft and four Whirlwind helicopters, along with two RAF Whirlwinds from No 22 Squadron. Damage caused by a storm in the North Atlantic necessitated repairs in Kingston, Jamaica. By the time they were complete, there was insufficient time to sail around Cape Horn, so she traversed the Panama Canal, passing through the narrowest locks with just inches to spare. HMS *Narvik* would reprise the role of control ship it had in Hurricane, but it was also required for Mosaic and had very little time to return to the Chatham Dockyard for a refit before heading out to Christmas Island for Grapple. In addition, there were the frigates HMS *Alert* and HMS *Cook*, and Royal New Zealand Navy frigates HMNZS *Pukaki* and *Rotoiti*.

The RAF and Royal Engineers improved the airfield to enable it to operate large, heavily loaded aircraft, and the port and facilities would be improved to enable Christmas Island to operate as a base by 1 December 1956. It was estimated that 18,640 measurement tons (21,110 $m^3$) of stores would be required for the construction effort alone. A dredge to clear the harbour was towed from Australia. Base development included improvements to the road system, and establishing an electricity supply, fresh water distillation plant, sewerage system and cold storage. The population of the island would peak at 3,000. The Army Task Group was commanded by Colonel J. E. S. 'Jack' Stone; Colonel John Woollett was the garrison commander.

The construction force was built around 38 Corps Engineer Regiment, with the 48, 59 and 61 Field Squadrons, and 63 Field Park Squadron, and 12 and 73 Independent Field Squadrons. Part of 25 Engineer Regiment also deployed. They were augmented by two construction troops from the Republic of Fiji Military Forces. With work on the plantations halted for the duration of Operation Grapple, the Gilbertese civilians were also employed on construction works and unloading the barges.

Our monitoring process was now in overdrive. We had medical records of some 30,000 people and were closely monitoring 500 people who were on our 'high risk' register. We needed a base in Fiji to ensure that the latest operational personnel were monitored; this would be added to our UK, America, Australia and New Zealand monitoring teams.

The troopship SS *Devonshire* sailed to the Central Pacific from East Asia. At Singapore she embarked 55 Field Squadron, which came from Korea, having been left behind there when the rest of 28 Engineer Regiment had returned to England after supporting the 1st Commonwealth Division in the Korean War. It also embarked Royal Marines Landing Craft Mechanized (LCM) crews from Poole. Heavy engineering plant and equipment was loaded on the SS *Reginald Kerr*, an LST converted to civilian use. *Devonshire* docked in Fiji, where it took on some sappers who had flown ahead, and an RAF medical team. *Devonshire* reached Christmas Island on 24 December, followed by *Reginald Kerr*, with Woollett on board. By the end of December 1956, there were nearly 4,000 personnel on Christmas Island, including two women from the Women's Voluntary Services.

Our team was sent to Christmas Island to ensure that medical records were kept correctly whilst the personnel were on the island and their duties were recorded and monitored correctly so we could work out NP ratings. Because of the significance of this task, I was sent to Christmas Island to implement the monitoring systems. I must add that I was not present during the tests; I left the island before any testing commenced to return to the UK to ensure that communications were established, and we could prepare for the documentation that was to be sent to us. We needed more storage space.

The first project, which was finished in October, was to rebuild the main runway at the airport to handle Valiants. This involved levelling a surface to extend it to 2,150 yards (1,970 m) long and 60 yards (55 m) wide. Some 20 miles (32 km) of access roads were built, and 700,000 square yards (590,000 sq m) of scrub were cleared. Existing buildings were refurbished, and new ones erected to provided 7,000 square yards (5,900 sq m) of building space. Twelve 105,000-imperial-gallon (480,000 l) storage tanks were provided for petrol, diesel and aviation fuel, along with pumping stations. The main camp consisted of over 700 tents and marquees, along with 40,000 square feet (3,700 sq m) of hutted accommodation. The airbase was ready to accommodate the Valiants and their crews by March 1957. The port was managed by 51 Port Detachment. No 504 Postal Unit, which had a detachment at Hickam Air Force Base, a United States Air Force (USAF) base in the American Territory of Hawaii, handled the receipt and despatch of mail, while No 2 Special Air Formation Signal Troop provided communications support. The Royal Army Service Corps provided a butchery, a bakery and a laundry. They also operated DUKWs, amphibious trucks which worked alongside the LCMs.

While Christmas Island was the main base, the area around Malden Island 400 nautical miles (740 km) to the south was to be the site for the bomber-dropped tests, and Penrhyn Island, 200 nautical miles (370 km) farther south, was used as a technical monitoring site and as a weather station. A USAF special weapons monitoring team was based here, and the airstrip was improved to allow its supporting Douglas C-124 Globemaster II to use it. A member of my team was also based there.

The Task Force received generous support from the United States Army, Navy and USAF. RAF aircraft were allowed to overfly the United States, even when carrying radioactive or explosive materials, thereby obviating the need for winterisation for the more northerly journey over Canada. RAF ground crews were accommodated at Hickam and Travis Air Force Base in California, and a regular aerial courier service operated from Hickam to Christmas Island. *Warrior* had repairs made at Pearl Harbour, and the US Army base at Fort DeRussy gave Woollett use of its facilities.

Having decided on a location and date, there still remained the matter of what would be tested. John Challens, whose weapons electronics group at Aldermaston had to produce the bomb assembly, wanted to know the configuration of Green Granite. Cook ruled that it would use a Red Beard Tom and would fit inside a Blue Danube casing for air dropping. The design was frozen in April 1956. There were two versions of Orange Herald, large and small. They had similar cores, but the large version contained more explosive. Both designs were frozen in July. The Green Bamboo design was also nominally frozen but tinkering with it continued. On 3 September, John Corner suggested that Green Granite could be made smaller by moving the Tom and Dick closer together. This design became known as Short Granite.

By January 1957, with the tests just months away, a tentative schedule had emerged. Short Granite would be fired first. Green Bamboo would follow if Short Granite was unsuccessful but be omitted as unnecessary otherwise. Orange Herald (small) would be fired next. Because Short Granite was too large to fit into a missile or guided bomb, this would occur whether or not Short Granite was a success. Finally, Green Granite would be tested. In December 1956, Cook had proposed another design, known as Green Granite II. This was smaller than Green Granite I and could fit into a Yellow Sun casing that could be used by the Blue Steel guided missile then under development; but it could not be made ready to reach Christmas Island before 26 June 1957 and extending Operation Grapple would cost another £1.5 million.

About 60 Gilbertese civilians were relocated to Fanning Island in January 1957 on the copra ship *Tungaru*, and another 40 on the *Tulgai* the following month. By mid-March, 44 Gilbertese men, 29 women and 56 children remained. By the end of April, 31 of the men, and all the women and children had been taken to Fanning Island by RAF Hastings. The civilians would remain there for the next three months, before returning to Christmas Island. During the later test series, the Gilbertese civilians remained on the island, marshalled in areas like the military personnel.

# Chapter 17 - Operation Grapple: The First Trials

I was flown back to the UK with my team remaining on the island. I had protested to my superiors as my previous aide had died after exposure to the tests and I did not want any more of my team exposed to this extremely powerful weapon and the fallout from it. I was assured that my team would be in protective clothing, at the farthest point from the detonation as possible. I was reassured and left the island. It was only later, when reviewing my team's monitoring files, that I found out they were not issued with protective clothing and stood with the rest of the personnel to watch the explosions. I was incensed by this but could do nothing at the time. Instead, I copied the files and waited.

The first trial series consisted of three shots. All bombs were dropped and detonated over Malden Island, and exploded high in the atmosphere, rather than being detonated on the ground, in order to reduce the production of nuclear fallout. British scientists were aware that the Americans had been able to reduce fallout by obtaining most of the bomb yield from fusion instead of fission, but they did not yet know how to do this. Amid growing public concern about the dangers of fallout, particularly from strontium-90 entering the food chain, a committee chaired by Sir Harold Himsworth was asked to look into the matter. Another committee in the United States, chaired by Detlev Bronk, also investigated. They reported simultaneously on 12 June 1956. While differing on many points, they agreed that levels of strontium-90 were not yet sufficiently high to be of concern.

At an altitude of 8,000 feet (2,400 m), the fireball would not touch the ground, thereby minimising fallout. The bombs would be detonated with a clockwork timer rather than a barometric switch. This meant that they had to be dropped from 45,000 feet (14,000 m). Grapple was Britain's second airdrop of a nuclear bomb after the Operation Buffalo test at Maralinga, and the first of a thermonuclear weapon. The United States had not attempted this until the Operation Redwing Cherokee test on 21 May 1956, and the bomb had landed 4 miles (6.4 km) from the target. Aldermaston wanted the bomb within 300 yards (270 m) of the target, and Oulton felt that a good bomber crew could achieve that. A 550-by-600-nautical-mile (1,020 by 1,110 km) exclusion zone was established, covering the area between 3.5° North and 7.5° South and 154° and 163° West, which was patrolled by Shackletons.

No 49 Squadron had eight Valiants, but only four deployed: XD818, piloted by Wing Commander Kenneth Hubbard, the squadron commander; XD822, piloted by Squadron Leader L. D. 'Dave' Roberts; XD823, piloted by Squadron Leader Arthur Steele; and XD824, piloted by Squadron Leader Barney Millett. The other four Valiants remained at RAF Wittering, where they were used as courier aircraft for bomb components. The last components for Short Granite were delivered by Valiant courier on 10 May 1957 – three days late owing to severe headwinds between San Francisco and Honolulu. A full-scale rehearsal was held on 11 May, and on 14 May it was decided to conduct the Grapple 1 test the following day. The eight official observers – two each from Australia, Canada, New Zealand and the United States – were flown from Honolulu to Christmas Island in a Handley Page Hastings, then to Malden Island in a Dakota, from whence a DUKW took them out to HMS *Alert*, the spectator ship. All but a small party were evacuated from Malden by HMS *Warrior*, *Narvik* and *Messina* by 19:00 on 14 May. The rest were picked up by a helicopter from *Warrior* at 07:45 on 15 May. Oulton and Cook arrived on Malden by Dakota at 08:25, where they were met by a helicopter and taken to *Narvik*.

One member of my team was present on the *Narvik* and witnessed the Grapple 1 test.

The Grapple 1 mission was flown by Hubbard in XD818, with Millett and XD824 as the 'grandstand' observation aircraft. The two bombers took off from Christmas Island at 09:00. The bomb was dropped from 45,000 feet (14,000 m) off the shore of Malden Island at 10:38 local time on 15 May 1957. Hubbard missed the target by 418 yards (382 m). The bomb's yield was estimated at 300 kilotonnes of TNT (1,300 TJ), far below its designed capability. Penney cancelled the Green Granite test and substituted a new weapon, codenamed Purple Granite. This was identical to Short Granite, but with some minor modification to its Dick; additional uranium-235 was added, and the outer layer was replaced with aluminium. Despite its failure, the test was hailed as a successful thermonuclear explosion, and the government did not confirm or deny reports that the UK had become a third thermonuclear power.

When documents on the series began to be declassified in the 1990s, the tests were denounced as a hoax intended to deceive the Americans into resuming nuclear cooperation; however, the reports would not have fooled the Americans observers, who helped to analyse samples from the radioactive cloud. I can inform you that they were not a hoax, the tests were real, and the documentation proves it. I have seen it and read it. This was a failed test, but it was a thermonuclear explosion.

The next test was Grapple 2, of Orange Herald (small). For this test, two Fijian official observers were added. A detachment of 39 Fijian Navy ratings who had been on board RNZN *Pukaki* and *Roititi* was transferred to HMS *Warrior*. This time there were also media representatives present on HMS *Alert*, including Chapman Pincher and William Connor. Orange Herald bomb components arrived in three separate loads on 13 May. Assembling them took two weeks. The bomb was dropped by XD822, piloted by Roberts. XD823, piloted by Steele, acted as the grandstand aircraft. This bomb was dropped at 10:44 local time on 31 May. After the bomb was released, Roberts made the standard 60° banked turn to get away, but his accelerometer failed, and the aircraft went into a high-speed stall. This was potentially disastrous, but through skilful flying Roberts was able to recover from the stall and use the mechanical accelerometer to complete the manoeuvre. The 720-800 kilotonne of TNT (3,000 to 3,300 TJ) yield was the largest ever achieved by a single stage device. This made it technically a megaton weapon; but it was close to Corner's estimate for an unboosted yield and there were doubts that the lithium-6 deuteride had contributed at all. This was chalked up to Taylor instability, which limited the compression of the light elements in the core.

The official release by the British government was that we had detonated a hydrogen bomb. Britain had become a nuclear power; we had succeeded where others had failed. The official classified reports show that it was a fission bomb and the British government lied to ensure that political eyes across the world were firmly on our testing programme. Such lies would continue until the present day.

The third and final shot of the series was Grapple 3, the test of Purple Granite. This was dropped on 19 June by a Valiant XD823 piloted by Steele, with Millett and XD824 as the grandstand aircraft. The yield was a very disappointing 300 kilotonnes of TNT (1,300 TJ), even less than Short Granite. The changes had not worked. "We haven't got it right," Cook told a flabbergasted Oulton. "We shall have to do it all again, providing we can do so before the ban comes into force; so that means as soon as possible."

So, Britain had not exploded a large-scale hydrogen bomb; the tests were not successful and, in fact, very disappointing. An emergency meeting of the NMC was convened in London, at which I was present.

"We need to demonstrate that we are a super power and have nuclear capability," was the opening statement of the meeting. "We need to do it at any cost. We cannot allow these failed tests to stop our work. We must continue and push harder – and we must do it now."

By now, our monitoring systems were so complex and so embedded into every test that the NMC were involved in all aspects of the tests. We were never asked for an opinion on the ethics of the tests or if we should carry on; we were just present and asked to provide the monitoring reports and ensure that the documentation was correct.

It was decided at that meeting to continue the Grapple series of tests. It was made clear there needed to be a successful test before any ban on testing was imposed.

# Chapter 18 - Operation Grapple X

The next test series consisted of a single trial known as Grapple X. To save time and money, and as HMS *Warrior*, *Alert* and *Narvik* were unavailable, it was decided to drop the bomb off the southern tip of Christmas Island rather than off Malden Island. This was just 20 nautical miles (37 km; 23 mi) from the airfield where 3,000 men were based. This required another major construction effort to improve the facilities on Christmas Island, and some of those that had been constructed on Malden Island had now to be duplicated on Christmas Island. Works included 26 blast-proof shelters, a control room, and tented accommodation. To provide some means of chasing away intruders, the destroyer HMS *Cossack* was allotted. HMNZS *Rotoiti* and *Pukaki* reprised their roles as weather ships. A cargo ship, the SS *Somersby,* was chartered to bring tentage and stores to Christmas Island. Monitoring equipment was set up on Malden Island and Fanning Island, and the observation posts on Penrhyn Island and Jarvis Island were re-established. Oulton noticed that:

*"The rumour had gone around the force that there were to be further tests and that they would have to remain much longer on Christmas. This was apparently confirmed by the preparations to build the air strip in the south of the island. The cheerful put-up-with-the-snags-and-get-on-with-this-important-job attitude of all ranks was changing to a sullen resentment. The troops of all three services had had a pretty miserable time, despite all efforts to the contrary, but had been buoyed up by the belief that the task was of great national importance and the sooner they got the three tests done, the sooner they could go home."*

This was confirmed in an official report that described the conditions that the personnel were enduring as very basic and worse than conditions during WW2 in some cases. Tent problems, food rationing, water issues and land crabs were causing major problems. Supplies were not reaching the personnel, and some were just barely surviving.

While some ships and units such as No 49 Squadron returned to the UK, most personnel had to remain on Christmas Island. The Minister of Supply gave assurances that no personnel would have to remain on the island for more than a year unless absolutely necessary, in which case home leave would be given. To maintain morale, units were given periodic briefings on the importance of their work. Junior officers took a keen interest in the welfare of the men and their families at home, since they were not permitted to bring them to the island. An efficient mail system was maintained to allow them to keep in contact. The quality of army rations was better than at any other British base. The men were given one day a week off work, and sports such as soccer, cricket, tennis, volleyball, sailing, fishing and water skiing were organised. Leave was provided that could be taken in Fiji, Hawaii or the Gilbert Islands. To relieve the monotony, some army personnel ashore exchanged places with navy personnel afloat. A Christmas Island Broadcasting Service was established with nightly radio programmes.

The scientists at Aldermaston had not yet mastered the design of thermonuclear weapons. Knowing that much of the yield of American and Soviet bombs came from fission in the uranium-238 tamper, they had focused on what they called the "lithium-uranium cycle", whereby neutrons from the fission of uranium would trigger fusion, which would produce more neutrons to induce fission in the tamper. However, this is not the most important reaction. Corner and his theoretical physicists at Aldermaston argued that Green Granite could be made to work by increasing compression and reducing Taylor instability. The first step would be achieved with an improved Tom. The Red Beard Tom was given an improved high explosive supercharge, a composite uranium-235 and plutonium core, and a beryllium tamper, thereby increasing its yield to 45 kilotonnes of TNT (190 TJ). The Dick was greatly simplified; instead of the 14 layers in Short Granite, it would have just three. This was called Round A; a five-layer version was also mooted, which was called Round B. A third round, Round C, was produced, which was a diagnostic round. It had the same three layers as Round A, but an inert layer instead of lithium deuteride. Grapple X would test Round A. Components of Rounds A and C were delivered to Christmas Island on

24, 27 and 29 October. On inspection, a fault was found in the Round A Tom, and the fissile core was replaced with the one from Round C.

This time there was no media presence, and only two foreign observers, Rear Admiral Patrick from the US Navy, and Brigadier General John W. White from the USAF. As the final preparations were being made for the test on 8 November, Oulton was advised at 01:00 that a Shackleton had sighted the SS *Effie*, an old Victory ship now flying the Liberian flag, in the exclusion zone. Eager to minimise publicity before this test, the British government had delayed sending out the Notice to Mariners, which had only been issued three weeks before. This failed to take into account the size of the Pacific Ocean; *Effie* had left its last port of call before it was issued. The Shackleton kept *Effie* under observation while trying to contact her, and *Cossack* was sent to intercept. By 06:00, all was in readiness for the test, but there was no news of *Effie*. Finally, at 06:15, word was received from the Shackleton that the crew had woken up and *Effie* had turned about and was now headed due south, out of the exclusion zone at 12 knots (22 km/h). A report from the Shackleton at 07:25 indicated that *Effie* was now sailing in company with *Cossack*.

By this time the Valiants had started their engines; they took off at 07:35 and were on the way when *Cossack* reported that *Effie* had cleared the area. The bomb was dropped from Valiant XD824, piloted by Millett, at 08:47 on 8 November 1957; Flight Lieutenant R. Bates flew the grandstand Valiant XD825. This time the yield of 1.8 megatonnes of TNT (7.5 PJ) exceeded expectations; the predicted yield had only been 1 megatonne (4.2 PJ). However, it was still below the 2 megatonnes (8.4 PJ) safety limit. This was the real hydrogen bomb Britain wanted, but it used a relatively large quantity of expensive highly enriched uranium. Due to the higher than expected yield of the explosion, there was some damage to buildings, the fuel storage tanks, and helicopters on the island.

My team were affected by this test; the building they were stationed in was damaged and they suffered minor injuries. The damage to the island was quickly fixed, but not before it was recorded by my team. Several personnel had experienced issues from the blast and needed treatment for various ailments. Unfortunately, no one had thought of the psychological impact that the tests would have on the personnel who watched the bomb drop and explode.

It was only years later that I witnessed this psychological damage when I attended a nuclear veterans' event. A video of the bomb was shown and the countdown to the explosion was heard. A number of veterans walked out, and one said, "I am sorry, I cannot stand to hear that again. I never want to hear that countdown."

Documentation was again stored as per our classifications and we ensured that our indexing system was still fit for purpose. We now had over 15,000 personnel records, as well as the records of the tests, recording of doses and fallout calculations.

The physicists at Aldermaston had plenty of ideas about how to follow up Grapple X. Possibilities were discussed in September 1957 at a special meeting of the NMC. This was a very technical meeting where detailed changes to the configuration were discussed. Even though I now had years of experience and an engineering degree, the calculations were beyond my comprehension.

One idea was to tinker with the width of the shells in the Dick to find an optimal configuration. If they were too thick, they would slow the neutrons generated by the fusion reaction; if they were too thin, they would give rise to Taylor instability. Another was to do away with the shells entirely and use a mixture of uranium-235, uranium-238 and deuterium. Ken Allen had an idea, which Samuel Curran supported, of a three-layer Dick that used lithium deuteride that was less enriched in lithium-6 (and therefore had more lithium-7), reducing the amount of uranium-235 in the centre of the core.

It took a month to come to a decision, but in October, Ken Allen's proposal was adopted, and it became known as "Dickens" because it used Ken's Dick. The device would otherwise be similar to Round A, but with a larger radiation case. The safety limit was again set to 2 megatonnes of TNT (8.4 PJ). Keith Roberts calculated that the yield could reach 3 megatonnes (13 PJ) and suggested that this could be reduced by modifying the tamper, but Cook opposed this, fearing that it might cause the test to fail. Because of the possibility of a moratorium on testing, plans for the test, codenamed Grapple Y, were restricted to the Prime Minister, who gave verbal approval, and a handful of officials.

I was one of six people in the UK who knew of the approval of the test, as we again had to implement monitoring procedures for the personnel on Christmas Island and back in the UK, where samples were returned for analysis.

The New Zealand National Party lost the 1957 election, and Walter Nash became Prime Minister. His New Zealand Labour Party had endorsed a call by the British Labour Party for a moratorium on nuclear testing, but he felt obligated to honour commitments made by his pre-decessors to support the British nuclear testing programme. However, HMNZS *Rotoiti* was unavailable, as it was joining the Far East Strate-gic Reserve; its place would be taken by the destroyer HMS *Ulysses*.

Air Vice Marshal John Grandy succeeded Oulton as Task Force Commander, and Air Commodore Jack Roulston became the Air Task Force Commander. The bomb was dropped off Christmas Island at 10:05 local time on 28 April 1958 by a Valiant piloted by Squadron Leader Bob Bates. It had an explosive yield of about 3 megatonnes of TNT (13 PJ), and remains the largest British nuclear weapon ever tested.

The design of Grapple Y was notably successful because much of its yield came from its thermonuclear reaction instead of fission of a heavy uranium-238 tamper, making it a true hydrogen bomb, and be-cause its yield had been closely predicted – indicating that its designers understood what they were doing.

The monitoring continued apace. The sheer size of the Grapple Y detonation meant all personnel on the island were affected and moni-toring was a 24/7 job.

On 22 August 1958, US President Dwight D. Eisenhower an-nounced a one-year moratorium on nuclear testing, effective 31 October 1958. Personally, I was delighted as it meant there would be no new personnel in our monitoring programme. Now we could enter into Phase 2 of our project, which was to monitor the existing subjects.

# Chapter 20 - Operation Grapple Z

I was summoned to an emergency meeting of the NMC to discuss the suspension of testing. I was expecting to be told that testing would cease and we could begin Phase 2 of the monitoring process; instead, I was disappointed to discover that the British government intended to perform as much testing as possible before the deadline.

The Soviet Union agreed to the deadline on 30 August. British scientists now needed to gather as much data as possible to allow them to design production nuclear weapons. As the prospect of increased American cooperation grew after October 1957, they knew that the quality and quantity of what the Americans would share would depend on what they had to offer. A new British test series, known as Grapple Z, was initiated. The number of tests in the Grapple Z series was assumed to be four for planning purposes, but as late as May the Prime Minister had only approved two shots, tentatively scheduled for 15 August and 1 September 1958. Four Valiants – XD818, XD822, XD824 and XD827 – deployed to Christmas Island, the last of which arrived on 31 July.

It would explore new technologies such as the use of external neutron initiators, which had first been tried out with Orange Herald. Core boosting using tritium gas and external boosting with layers of lithium deuteride permitted a smaller, lighter Tom for two-stage devices. It would be the biggest and most complex British test series yet.

Of particular concern was radiation damage, known as the RI effect. Keith Roberts and Bryan Taylor at Aldermaston had discovered that the flash of radiation from the detonation of an atomic bomb could affect a nearby bomb. This opened up the possibility of a missile warhead being disabled by another launched for this purpose. Plutonium cores were especially vulnerable, as they were already prone to pre-detonation. This had the potential to render Britain's nuclear deterrent ineffective. The discovery was given the highest level of secrecy, and Aldermaston would spend many of the next few years working on the problem. To build a primary immune to this effect would require techniques that Aldermaston had not yet mastered.

Again, representatives of my team were to be deployed to the island. I discouraged anyone from returning as I did not want them to participate in more than one test. However, it was difficult to stop people from going; after all, a trip across the world to an island paradise was on offer – who would not want to go? In vain, I tried to make them understand the dangerous nature of this experiment and that things could go wrong. There was no shortage of volunteers for the trip.

The first shot was a test of Pendant, a fission bomb boosted with solid lithium hydride intended as a primary for a thermonuclear bomb. Rather than being dropped from a bomber, this bomb was suspended from a string of four vertically stacked barrage balloons. This was chosen over an air drop because the bomb assembly could not be fitted into a droppable casing, but it introduced a host of problems. A balloon shot had been tried only once before by the British, during Operation Antler at Maralinga in October 1957. William Saxby from Aldermaston was placed in charge of the balloon crews, who commenced training at RAF Cardington in Bedfordshire in January 1958. Inflating the balloons required 1,200 cylinders of hydrogen gas, and there were no reserves. If another balloon test was required, then the empty cylinders would have to be returned to the United Kingdom for refilling, and then shipped out again. An important consideration was how they could be shot down if they broke loose of their moorings with a live hydrogen bomb. The cargo ship SS *Tidecrest* arrived at Christmas Island on 20 July, but the firing harness was lost at San Francisco International Airport on 1 August, and a replacement had to be flown out. The Pendant fissile core arrived by air on 12 August, and the weapon was assembled with its external neutron initiator unit. On 22 August 1958 it was lifted 1,500 feet (460 m) in the air, and it detonated at 09:00. The yield was assessed at 24 kilotonnes of TNT (100 TJ).

The next shot was of Flagpole, an unboosted version of Orange Herald known as Indigo Herald. It was air dropped by Valiant XD822, flown by Squadron Leader Bill Bailey, with XD818 flown by Flight Lieutenant Tiff O'Connor as the grandstand aircraft, on 2 September

1958. This was the first live drop of a British nuclear weapon using blind radar technique. Bailey managed to put the bomb 95 yards (87 m) from the target. It detonated at 8,500 feet (2,600 m) at 08:24 with a yield of about 1.2 megatonnes of TNT (5.0 PJ).

The third shot was of Halliard, an unusual three-stage design with two nuclear-fission components followed by a thermonuclear stage that was supposedly immune to exposure from another bomb despite its not using boosting. The Americans had indicated an interest in it. Macmillan noted in his diary:

*"Meeting of atomic experts just returned from US. Two important facts emerged: (a) Americans are doing ten more kiloton tests before the end of October and would not wish us to stop before them; (b) in some respects we are as far, and even further, advanced in the art than our American friends. They thought interchange of information would be all give. They are keen that we should complete our series, especially the last megaton, the character of which is novel and of deep interest to them. This is important, because it makes this final series complementary rather than competitive – and therefore easy to defend in Parliament."*

The success of blind bombing in Flagpole led to Grandy deciding to use the blind radar technique again. Hubbard was less sure. In 52 practice drops with blind radar, the average error had been 235 yards (215 m) as opposed to 245 yards (224 m) with visual bombing. The problem for the aircrew was that they would be dropping a live hydrogen bomb – generally considered a dangerous thing to do – with no means of verifying that their instruments were correct.

Can you imagine being asked to drop a live hydrogen bomb using a blind radar technique? These days we have complex satellite imaging, GPS instruments, digital tracking and remote control. Then, there was nothing but the skills of the crew.

Air Chief Marshal Sir Harry Broadhurst, the head of Bomber Command, wished O'Connor luck; his XD827 would make the drop, with Squadron Leader Tony Caillard in XD827, the grandstand aircraft. The aircraft took off at 07:15 on 11 September 1958. Once in the air, though, a fault developed in the ground radar transmitter. Grandy then authorised a visual drop. It was later confirmed that it was 260 yards (240 m) from the target. It was detonated at 8,500 feet (2,600 m) at 08:49 with a yield of about 800 kilotonnes of TNT (3,300 TJ), very close to the predicted yield of 750 kilotonnes (3,100 TJ).

In the years since this test, I have seen the documented report on the decision to change to a visual drop. The lives of the men on the island were put into the hands of the crew of this Valiant aircraft. One wrong decision could have led to serious consequences. The pressure put on this crew was ridiculous; it is extremely hard to imagine what you would do in their position. We did not record any conversations within the aircraft, but I am sure it was interesting!

The final test in the Grapple Z series was of Burgee, at 09:00 on 23 September 1958. This was another balloon-borne test. Burgee was an atomic bomb boosted with gaseous tritium created by a generator codenamed Daffodil. It had a yield of about 25 kilotonnes of TNT (100 TJ). The Aldermaston weapon makers had now demonstrated all the technologies that were needed to produce a megaton hydrogen bomb that weighed no more than 1 long ton (1.0 t) and was immune to premature detonation caused by nearby nuclear explosions. The international moratorium commenced on 31 October 1958, and Britain never resumed atmospheric testing.

This end to the testing was a relief for my team. We could now enter the next stage of the project – but a holiday was needed before Phase 2 commenced.

# Chapter 21 – The One Who Didn't Make It

Years after the testing programme, I had a chance encounter with an RAF pilot who told me that he felt he was the luckiest man on earth. I asked him why he felt this way. This is his story:

*"I was en route to Christmas Island; I had been tasked with flying a Valiant over the island to collect the fallout from the detonations. The plane had been modified to allow for the fallout to be collected and I would receive my orders once I reached Hawaii.*

*During a short stay in Hawaii, I became seriously ill with appendicitis and needed to have my appendix removed. This meant that I could not meet the deadline to fly into the cloud and we needed to seek a replacement for me.*

*I was sent to an American army base for the emergency operation. Once I had recovered from the operation, I was sent back to the UK.*

*My replacement died of cancer in his 50s. I have now researched the tests myself and can see that several personnel and their families claim to be affected by the tests.*

*I was so close to being there and in the fallout cloud. Someone must have been watching over me."*

I could not tell him at the time that he would have been classified as a 1NP1 member of the tests. I had seen his file and he was in fact very lucky. His rating was unique in the entire file, for he was now classed an ONDP1, which stood for No Direct Participation. We kept his 1 rating as his role would have been at the highest level of exposure.

This man does not know the full extent of the testing programme and its effects on the personnel involved in the tests. I do. He may as well have won the lottery that day as he suffered no ill effects and went on to have a very successful career in the Air Force and, later, in private aviation.

I once asked a nuclear veteran at a conference, "Would you have gone to the island if you knew what was going to happen?" He stood in front of me and started to cry. This was a man in his 70s who had faced lots of enemies in his career, been shot at and endured many campaigns.

*"No way would I have gone if they had told me and I knew the effects on my family. I would never have got on the plane. I would rather have gone AWOL."*

His daughter was born with multiple deformities and problems and he attributed it to the tests. He himself has undergone various cancer treatments and had tumours removed.

*"I sit and watch my daughter in a wheelchair struggle every day and think, 'Was it me? Did those tests affect me, and I passed it onto her?' I am still struggling with this every day."*

# Chapter 22 – Documenting Grapple

My team returned to the UK and we again collated the thousands of monitoring reports relating to the X, Y and Z tests. The task was immense; we were receiving daily reports relating to medical issues, marriages, miscarriages, deformities in children and suicides.

Each person had their files logged and classified and they were stored within the dedicated vaults at GCHQ. (We now had outgrown the initial vault and were onto our second storage vault.) A new indexing system was needed for Phase 2 and a new coding system was added to the initial code.

As per our initial coding system, we tried to keep it simple. We already had the following codes:

- Number of tests
- Nuclear Participant (NP)
- A 1-10 scale of the exposure level (according to the role of the person)
- Any cobalt exposure
- A 1-10 scale of the cobalt exposure

An example is 1NP1C1 which stood for 1 test, Nuclear Participant, highest exposure, cobalt exposure at the highest level.

As we did not have complex database systems and indexing programmes which would allow us to retrieve records in seconds, we needed to ensure we captured each incident. It was decided to add single letters to the coding system for the following events:

M = Married (again with a number for multiple marriages)

L = Loss of a child through miscarriage (again with a number)

S = Suicide

X = Cancer treatment

K = Children (again with a number)

D = Deformities of a child (linked to the K code)

T = Stillborn child (linked to the K Code)

Z = Death (alongside their age)

Attached to each main personnel record would also be their spouse's record and any children's records, all using the same new coding system. We were preparing to monitor grandchildren and, potentially, great grandchildren.

I remember these codes as if it were yesterday. When a file was pulled from the vault to add another incident, I would look at the front cover and the code attached and be dismayed by the number of records where the codes were increasing. The numbers were increasing at an alarming rate.

I decided to split my team into multiple sections, one dealing with health, one with marriages, one with deaths and another with children.

Where personnel had film badges attached to them, the dosages had been recorded in the file; otherwise, they had been estimated according to role and location. I once asked where the film badges were as some personnel who had been allocated them only seemed to have an estimated reading. I was told that the badges had malfunctioned and had been destroyed.

# Chapter 23 – The 1958 US-UK Mutual Defence Agreement

British timing was good. The Soviet Union's launch of Sputnik 1, the world's first artificial satellite, on 4 October 1957 came as a tremendous shock to the American public, who had trusted that American technological superiority ensured their invulnerability. Now, suddenly, there was incontrovertible proof that, in some areas at least, the Soviet Union was actually ahead. In the widespread calls for action in response to the Sputnik crisis, officials in the United States and Britain seized an opportunity to mend the relationship that had been damaged by the Suez Crisis. At the suggestion of Harold Caccia, the British Ambassador to the United States, Macmillan wrote to Eisenhower on 10 October urging that the two countries pool their resources to meet the challenge. To do this, the McMahon Act's restrictions on nuclear cooperation needed to be relaxed.

British information security, or the lack thereof, no longer seemed so important now that the Soviet Union was apparently ahead, and the United Kingdom had independently developed the hydrogen bomb. The trenchant opposition from the Joint Committee on Atomic Energy that had derailed previous attempts was absent. Amendments to the Atomic Energy Act of 1954 passed Congress on 30 June 1958 and were signed into law by Eisenhower three days later. The 1958 US–UK Mutual Defence Agreement was signed on 3 July and approved by Congress on 30 July. Macmillan called this "the Great Prize".

My preparations for Phase 2 and the shutdown of Phase 1 were premature. I was again summoned to a meeting of the NMC and told: "We have entered into this agreement and will be participating in further tests. You need to ensure that any British personnel are monitored to the same standard as the previous tests. The numbers will be significantly lower, but we will have to co-operate with the Americans." I was dismayed. My new structure within the department had to be ripped apart and again we geared up for more testing.

I flew to America to discuss the monitoring that was being

performed by the American government and was surprised to find that they had adopted my system, which had been disclosed to them. This made it easier for us to work with their monitoring systems.

The tests were scheduled for 1962 and were to be undertaken by Joint Task Force 8. With testing taking place on Johnston Island and Christmas Island in the Pacific, my team were on their travels again.

This time one of my officials wanted to attend. He had already attended two tests and his request was refused. I did not want him to attend a third test, especially as this operation would consist of 31 nuclear explosions.

# Chapter 24 – Operation Dominic

Operation Dominic occurred during a period of high Cold War tension between the United States and the Soviet Union, since the Cuban Bay of Pigs Invasion had occurred not long before. Nikita Khrushchev announced the end of the three-year moratorium on nuclear testing on 30 August 1961, and Soviet testing recommenced on 1 September, initiating a series of tests that included the detonation of the Tsar Bomb. President John F. Kennedy responded by authorizing Operation Dominic. It was to be the largest nuclear weapons testing programme ever conducted by the United States and the last atmospheric test series conducted by the US, as the Limited Test Ban Treaty was signed in Moscow the following year.

These latest tests, which had a combined yield of 38.1 megatonnes, were scheduled quickly, in order to respond in kind to the Soviet resumption of testing after the moratorium. Most of these shots were conducted with free-fall bombs dropped from B-52 bomber aircraft. Twenty of these shots were to test new weapons designs; six to test weapons effects; and several shots to confirm the reliability of existing weapons. The Thor missile was also used to lift warheads into near-space to conduct high-altitude nuclear explosion tests; these shots were collectively called Operation Fishbowl.

The operation started on 25 April 1962 with the Adobe test, with a yield of 190 kilotonnes; the largest test was Housatonic, with a yield of 8,300 kilotonnes. The final test was completed on 4 November 1962.

British personnel from the combined services participated in the tests, helping the Americans and ensuring that the results of the tests were jointly analysed to the mutual benefit of both countries.

My team worked well with the American monitoring team. Once again, we collated information in the same format as the Operation Grapple tests, but on a smaller scale in terms of personnel. What we were not told was that there would be 36 tests in 9 months. My team was pushed to the limit; the timescale was difficult to meet. I was contacted by a senior member of my team who asked for more personnel.

I decided to attend the last 10 tests on the island to help with the monitoring process. I had chosen to witness the largest test of the series, and one of the most powerful weapons ever detonated. It was a frightening experience, but to my surprise, the British personnel had become nonchalant to the tests and continued about their work as if there were nothing going on. I spoke to one of the servicemen, whose response was: "We have got used to the tests now. We used to retreat to safe locations as per the American personnel; we just return to our bunks now and relax until it is over."

They had no idea of the risks that they were exposing themselves to. By now, I had seen thousands of reports and was extremely worried for their future. How many would make it past their fifties? How many would have children who had health issues or would die young?

I felt like the lab technician dealing with mice who knew that the mice were going to suffer and die but continued to experiment on them.

# Chapter 25 – Updating Government Departments

We returned from Operation Dominic and were immediately tasked to report our findings to the various government departments. It was a very busy time for us: the Dominic tests had occurred in such a short space of time, we had an indexing problem to solve.

At the same time, microfiche was being introduced around the world, and I investigated it as a solution to our storage issues. It was decided that we would microfiche all our records to enable them to be stored more easily than paper records. This was a major undertaking for my department.

I again split the teams into the Phase 2 sections and added more personnel to microfiche the records. I now had 150 people under my command.

We were receiving daily reports from the other departments across the world. We now had a problem though: personnel were leaving the service and returning to civilian life after National Service. We now had to include any hospital, GP or consultant across the world that treated the servicemen so our records would be correct.

An emergency meeting was held of the NMC. I wanted to close down the project; we had the records, the exposure and the details of the roles of the personnel so why did we need to monitor it further? It was getting out of control and I was concerned that our record keeping, which, until now, had been extremely accurate, would not continue as per my standards.

Under order from the Prime Minister, I contacted each British embassy across the world and informed them of the monitoring actions. This was completed in such a way that the embassy officials did not learn about our project; we just wanted to ensure that no matter where in the world these people settled, their medical details were tagged.

Any person resettling overseas would have their records tagged in the respective country and reported to us as per our standard monitoring process. It was accepted that a few countries could not complete this monitoring to the UK standards, especially those lacking enough internal systems to monitor the personnel.

We were now in Phase 2 of the project, with monitoring systems implemented, and reports classified and microfiched as per our procedures. We were starting to build a database of the effects of nuclear testing on over 24,000 people.

# Chapter 26 – The First Issues

We started to receive reports of suicides amongst the highest-level personnel; one pilot who had been exposed not once but twice flying a 'hot' aircraft had committed suicide. I attended a meeting of the NMC and we were told that we were being re-classified from a monitoring department that filed reports to an investigative department that needed to work with MI5; we would now come under the command of the Joint Intelligence Committee (JIC).

I was asked to head up the new department and we were given the codename NIA, which stood for Nuclear Intelligence Agency. Our brief to record and monitor the personnel was expanded to include investigating issues, visiting personnel and ensuring that any information regarding the tests was not disclosed under any circumstances.

I was now in my fifties and contemplated leaving the project, but I was offered a knighthood for my services and my salary doubled. Thinking of my pension and retirement, I took the job offer. This was the worst decision of my life. I had entered the world of espionage and deceit. A world where government departments cover up incidents and deny all responsibility. A world in which I no longer had any control. I was ordered to perform several tasks I did not want to perform, but was duty bound to do so.

One such task – the first under my new role – was the worst experience of my life.

We had received a report from a hospital of a stillborn baby who had severe deformities. I was tasked with visiting the hospital and impersonating a doctor so I could talk to the parents and see if they were connecting the birth with the nuclear tests the father had been involved in.

I retrieved his file and found that he was a 1NP1C1L2T, the highest level that we could attribute. There were already two miscarriages assigned to his record and now a stillborn child.

The couple were distraught when I arrived at the hospital. I was not an agent of the government; I was simply an engineer who had implemented the monitoring systems. I spoke to the couple and was convinced that at this time (early 1960s) they had not attributed the death of their child to the tests. The government plan of not releasing information was working at this early stage.

As I was leaving the hospital, I was approached by another civil servant who I had not met before. "I need your assistance in this matter," he said. "We are going to store the deformed child in our medical archives. We need to study this baby for future reference."

I almost collapsed. "You want to do what?" I replied. It was immoral.

They had not asked for the couple's consent. There was to be no funeral or ceremony. The baby was to become an experiment in this monitoring study.

That night, I was sick to my stomach. What had I become involved in? Keeping records was one thing; keeping babies was another. I had not signed up for this and I thought things could not get worse. How wrong I was.

# Chapter 27 – The Veterans

We continued to monitor the records and our investigative department continued to impersonate officials. If a medical professional was interested in the effects of the tests and details had been recorded on the subject's files, they were visited by the team and told not to progress it any further. In some cases, the official was removed from their post immediately and relocated.

The veterans were now becoming suspicious and several articles were starting to appear in the papers regarding the nuclear tests. By now we were into the late 1970s and the participants of the nuclear tests were joining forces in order to campaign for justice. They were becoming more and more professional and in 1983, they formed an Association with multiple branches across the UK.

Data was being collated by the veterans on deaths and family issues. Data that we already had but had never disclosed.

My department, the NIA, held an emergency meeting. We needed to ensure that the veterans did not get their hands on any of our records; we could not be infiltrated in any way. Personnel within my department had seen hundreds of sensitive documents. All personnel that had worked in my department were to be visited and their responsibility under the Official Secrets Act was to be reiterated. No one from my team was to disclose any information we had been privy to.

I argued at the meeting that my team were professionals; why did they need to be reminded? What was the government scared of? Why did they feel the need to protect the records and the information held within the archives?

I was informed that the British government was becoming increasingly worried by the reports my department were generating on a regular basis about the increasing health effects not just on the personnel involved but also their families. We knew the personnel had been exposed, but new technologies were emerging and with better diagnosis of conditions, the government was worried about compensation claims from the veterans, especially through the newly formed British

Nuclear Test Veterans Association.

We were already at the highest classification level for our records, but security was tightened even further.

I was now head of an MI5 department whose responsibility was to protect the files and to ensure that no one was in receipt of any information relating to the catastrophic effect of the nuclear tests. I was effectively protecting information which would help the personnel involved; I was to deny all knowledge. All to protect the government from compensation claims by the veterans. It all came down to money. But how much was being spent protecting the files? Why not come clean?

# Chapter 28 - McClelland Royal Commission

Following the initial clean-up of Maralinga in 1967, pressure had mounted mounting regarding the after-effects of the tests. Media reports led to public outcry about the increasing evidence (and statistical significance) of premature deaths among former Australian staff associated with the atomic tests and subsequent birth defects in their offspring. Likewise, remote indigenous communities downwind of the tests had statistically significant higher rates of radiation-related diseases not generally found to the same level among such communities. In light of the increasing evidence and public lobbying by concerned groups, in 1984 the Hawke Labour Government established a Royal Commission to investigate the British atomic tests in Australia.

The Royal Commission into nuclear tests was told that 30 badly leaking drums of radioactive waste had been dumped off the West Australian coast. The Commission was also told that acting Prime Minister Arthur Fadden had sent a message to the British PM asking, "What the bloody hell is going on? The cloud is drifting over the mainland!"

I was aware of these leaking barrels; they had been reported to me years before. Documented minutes of meetings of the NIA dismissed the discovery and we were told to deny any knowledge.

The McClelland Royal Commission was told that one hundred Aboriginal people had walked barefoot over nuclear-contaminated ground because boots they had been given didn't fit. According to a scientist who was involved in the tests, the 1953 British nuclear test that allegedly caused the 'black mist' phenomenon in South Australia should not have been fired and the fallout was about three times more than forecast.

I had full evidence of this. The fallout was 2.9 times more than forecast and the 'black mist' had indeed happened. Our reports showed that even though we knew not to detonate the device, we carried on.

A house built less than 200 metres from an area mined for mineral sands 25 years ago was still contaminated from mineral-sands tailings which were dangerously radioactive. According to a special report into an investigation of residual radioactive contamination, about 100,000 dangerous metal fragments contaminated with plutonium still littered the Maralinga atomic test range – 25 years after the atomic tests that caused them.

A mechanical engineer told the Commission that Geiger counter readings of the fallout levels near Marble Bar were "off-the-scale".

The McClelland Royal Commission found that:

- Then Australian Prime Minister Sir Robert Menzies approved the British nuclear tests without first receiving independent Australian scientific advice on the hazards to humans or the environment.

- The Australia Federal Cabinet was kept in the dark by Menzies about key aspects of the nuclear tests.

- The atomic test agreement by the British and Australian governments was done in retrospect after the first test had occurred.

- Australia was forced to accept UK assurances on the safety and likely fallout lifespan hazards of the atomic tests, without an independent scientific assessment.

- Australia's key representative to oversee the atomic tests, Sir Ernest Titterton, was in fact a British ex-pat who withheld key information from the Australian government.

- The safeguards against radiation exposure for the nuclear veterans were totally inadequate, even by the best practice standards of the 1950s.

- It is probable that the rate of cancers that occurred subsequent to the testing would not otherwise have occurred were it not for the fallout from the tests.

- The Vixen tests on plutonium should have not occurred, even with the limited 1950s knowledge of the half-life and radiation hazards.

- Failure to provide Australian air crews with protective equipment on over-flights or direct fly-throughs of the atomic mushroom clouds was clearly negligent.

An urgent meeting of the NIA was sanctioned. The inquiry had highlighted the issues we had been hiding for nearly 30 years. I was asked at the meeting to provide documentary evidence of these findings. My team worked through the night to find the documents, copy them and present them to the NIA board.

When we realised the report was in fact correct in 90% of its findings, we were faced with a difficult decision: should we admit that there were problems with the tests or deny any responsibility? If we admitted responsibility, the floodgates would open. The financial pay-outs would cripple the already stretched government finances.

We were to pass our findings on to Lorna Arnold, who would prepare the British government's official response to the Commission's report. Arnold was a historian who had written several books on the British nuclear tests and had been the UKAEA records officer.

The Commission's report and conclusions differed wildly from Arnold's treatise, "A Very Special Relationship: British Atomic Weapon Trials in Australia". Her report emphasized the partnership between the two nations and noted that the approach taken towards safety was to international standards of the time and had contrasted with the historic disregard of Australian authorities toward the welfare of indigenous people.

Some observers have noted that both reports were framed in the politics of the time: Britain wished to minimize its responsibility, while the Australian government of Bob Hawke wished to implicate their political opponents alongside the British. It has been suggested that the timeline of the inquiry was chosen so as not to implicate earlier Labour governments.

However, it should be noted that the Australian Labour Party had not been in power federally from 1950 until 1972, clearly undermining that argument. Likewise, the Arnold report was criticized for being authored by a former employee of the United Kingdom Atomic Energy Authority (UKAEA), and for the author having never visited the test sites nor interviewed Australian participants who worked on the atomic tests.

The Royal Commission witness statements of discussions between Australian RAAF and USAF B-29 flight crews clearly demonstrate that the tests were not at then international standards in terms of testing instruments nor health and safety precautions for radiation.

The Royal Commission heard ample evidence of British scientists being fully dressed in protective radiation suits that were not issued to Australian staff working in the same high-risk radiation zones. Overall, the Arnold argument that the British nuclear tests were carried out in partnership with Australia was not compatible with the documented facts that the British controlled and managed the tests and the Australians worked under the direction of British atomic test leaders.

The Commission report was the first that had challenged our own records but we had succeeded in ensuring the secrets contained within the vaults remained safe.

Debate continued over the safety of the Maralinga site and the long-term health effects on both the traditional Aboriginal custodians of the land and former test personnel. In 1994, the Australian government agreed to compensation amounting to $13.5 million to the local Maralinga Tjarutja people.

The British government contributed to these costs, paying the full $13.5 million to the Tjarutja people. It was a payoff for their silence, for the British government wanted to ensure that no further investigations or enquiries into the Maralinga test site would be completed. Measures were taken, however, to perform a further clean-up of the site; this was completed in 2000 at a cost of $108 million – of which Britain paid half.

At the meeting of the NIA that debated this compensation agreement, there was initially some trepidation about making the payment. Would it pave the way for affected British personnel to mount their own compensation claims? However, it was deemed that the tests had contaminated the land, not the people, effectively meaning British personnel could not claim anything from the government.

There was also a fear that the inhabitants of Christmas Island may also launch a challenge to the testing programme and claim compensation, so money was allocated for a clean-up there.

Once again, the serving personnel of the British Armed Forces were to be discounted. Mounting evidence of illness, death and deformities was being ignored. Rather than tackle the problem, it was buried in the archives.

# Chapter 29 – 1985: My Retirement

In 1985, I was to turn 65 and therefore retire from my post as head of the NIA. I had seen so many terrible reports, experienced nuclear explosions, seen friends and colleagues die from their exposure – and had the evidence to prove it.

I had seen cover-ups and been involved in the most terrible operations involving recovering dead children, impersonating officials and lying to our veterans. The time was right for me to go.

I attended what I thought was a handover meeting to my second-in-command and was then asked to speak to the Prime Minister and several senior officials. I was thanked for my service and was to receive a handsome payoff and a good pension. I was looking forward to retiring in South Wales; I had purchased a house on the coast years earlier in preparation for this day.

"We want to you to stay on as an advisor." The words rang in my ears. Just like the personnel involved, I was never to be free of this testing programme.

I did not want to be involved in the NIA any longer, but I was reminded of my responsibilities and told that my experience and knowledge was invaluable to the government and I was needed to advise the senior officials on the archives.

I really had no choice. I had heard of other officials who had turned down the offer of advisory roles, only to die soon after retirement, through car crashes or just natural causes. I did not want this to happen to me, so I accepted the position on the understanding that it would be no more than 40 days per year.

I needed a break from the NIA, so I returned to South Wales and enjoyed a few days' holiday before taking a cruise in the Caribbean.

It was during this cruise that I received word that the veterans of the nuclear tests had now set up branches across the country. Their numbers were increasing and their voice was starting to be heard. They were co-ordinating their efforts and had a very vocal spokesman who was discussing pensions and illnesses and calling on the government to look after them.

This was a new phase in the programme. We had not anticipated that the veterans would co-ordinate their efforts and form an Association. New monitoring systems were to be implanted to ensure that their efforts did not reveal the truth.

We needed to ensure that we had some documented reports that would allow us to fight any claims made by the veterans and their families; we needed to compile evidence that would stand up in court.

At a meeting of the NIA in 1983, scientists from the National Radiological Protection Board (NRPB) and the Imperial Cancer Research Fund (now Cancer Research UK) were commissioned by the Ministry of Defence (MoD) to carry out an independent epidemiological study of participants in the UK atmospheric nuclear weapons tests, both in the Pacific and in Australia.

The NRPB had expertise in epidemiological research of radiation-exposed populations and an interest in furthering the knowledge of health effects of human exposure to radiation. As a non-departmental public body, it was able to conduct research and to publish findings independently. The combination of our database, the statistical and epidemiological expertise of the researchers and access to NRPB colleagues such as radiation physicists, chemists and biologists meant the research was able to cover a wide range of relevant issues. (The functions of the NRPB has since been transferred to Public Health England (PHE), who continue to manage the study.)

Beginning in 1983 and continuing to this day, the Nuclear Weapons Test Participants Study (NWTPS) is described as "a long-term follow up study of the health of UK personnel who were present at UK atmospheric tests conducted between 1952 and 1967."

The NWTPS is an epidemiological study, meaning it collects data on people's exposure to particular events and the occurrence of particular diseases in those people. Statistical analysis compares those exposed with those who are not exposed to see if there is any difference in the pattern of diseases.

The NWTPS took a group of people who were present at the UK atmospheric nuclear tests and compares them with the general population and with another similar group of people who were not at the tests (a control group). The study examines whether there are significant differences in mortality causes or cancer incidence between these groups.

Participants in the nuclear weapons test programme would have differed in some ways from men of the same age in the general UK population. For example, test participants needed to have been fit enough to be selected for overseas service, and they would have experienced a different lifestyle during their period in a tropical or desert environment. Consequently, as well as comparing mortality and cancer rates among test participants with the corresponding national rates, comparisons were also made with the control group.

The control group contains roughly the same number of men as the participants' group and, apart from not participating in the tests, the controls were chosen to have similar characteristics to the participants. For test participants in the armed forces, the controls were selected from service personnel who served in tropical or sub-tropical areas other than the test locations around the time that the tests were taking place.

For AWE (Atomic Weapons Establishment) test participants, the controls were chosen from other men working for AWE at around the same time as the weapons tests. The 22,333 men in the control group were very similar to the participants with respect to the split between services, ranks or social class, year of birth, year of enlistment or employment and year of discharge or end of employment.

The NWTPS study aimed to include all UK personnel from the RAF, the Army, the Royal Navy, AWE or UKAEA (UK Atomic Energy Authority) who had had potential for exposure to radiation as a result of involvement in the nuclear weapon test programmes in Australia or the Christmas Island region between 1952 and 1967.

As there was not thought to be a complete list of those who visited test sites during the programmes, the study group was identified following the examination of an extensive range of documents, including planning documents, technical reports, health records, Royal Navy ships' ledgers and RAF operational record books as well as service records and other documents.

Of course, we did have a complete list of the participants of the programme – we had extensive records and evidence – but we could not state this. If we disclosed that we had details of every single participant at the tests, their partners, families and full medical details, it would be catastrophic to any claim against us. The government needed to emphasise that the study was only based on those participants that could be identified by the available documents.

Employees of many other organisations were involved in the test programmes (the Meteorological Office and the Merchant Navy, for example), but the records available to the researchers in 1983 were not sufficiently complete to allow identification of the relevant individuals and so these groups were not included in the NWTPS study group. Foreign personnel were not included either, as health follow-up for non-UK personnel could not be ascertained in the same way as for UK personnel.

Additionally, it was also decided to exclude the very few women who had taken part in the tests as the number was too small for useful analysis. The exclusion of records from the study does not mean that the individuals are necessarily different to those included in the study, rather that the data was not sufficiently complete to add value to the epidemiological work.

There is a dilemma in defining the population to be studied. On the one hand, if it included only those clearly likely to be exposed to radiation (for example, aircrew sampling the radioactive plumes from the explosions), then it would exclude other groups who should also be regarded as bona fide test participants. On the other hand, including as many as possible of those involved in the tests would inevitably include some groups who had little real chance of having been exposed and might dilute away any excess of disease in those most at risk. To try to deal with this issue, the investigators took a wide definition of test participation but also carried out special analyses of those sub-groups which might have been at increased risk.

The 2003 report detailed the study cohort of 21,357 participants; completeness checks undertaken by the researchers indicate that this represents 85% of the total eligible study population. It was not necessary to include all test participants in the study, though it was desirable that as many of them as possible were included. A larger study population increases the ability to detect any harmful effect of test participation. It was, however, important for the study team to ascertain whether the 15% not included were not significantly different to those included with regard to their potential exposure to radiation and their health.

The NRPB researchers were also able to assemble a list of test participants from sources independent of the MoD. When the researchers looked within this independently compiled list, they found that the health experience of those also found in the MoD records was similar to the health experience of the 15% who were not included. This provided powerful evidence against the idea that less healthy individuals were less likely to be included in the study population.

As the study continued, the researchers were unwilling to include additional records to the study cohort because they did not want to introduce 'bias' to the study. For example, if they added details of those men who confirmed that they had been present this could distort the findings because those who had already died could not contact the researchers.

We received numerous calls relating to the study asking why people had not been included. Our response was if they could not be identified, they were excluded. Of course, they could be identified; we just chose not to identify them.

At the time of the last analysis, carried out in 2003, only 4,902 (23%) of the 21,357 study participants were known to have died. Some had emigrated but the majority, 14,560 (68%) were still alive. As nuclear weapons test participants were adults in the 1950s and 1960s, even the youngest of them would, by the year 2000, have been aged over 50. Those aged in their later twenties or older at the time of the earliest test, in 1952, would have been at least in their seventies by the year 2000. The life expectancy of a boy born in 1930 was less than 60 years so it is not surprising that an increasing number of former test participants are no longer alive.

Information about health events (such as date and causes of death, and date and details of cancer incidence information) are provided to the study team by the NHS Central Registers (NHSCRs). The NWTPS examines all causes of death, whether from cancer or any other disease or condition. The NWTPS reports show more details. The UK national registries are internationally recognised as an invaluable resource in providing excellent and unbiased information about deaths and cancers in the UK population. There is no better resource available for this type of study.

Before 1971, there was no UK-wide system for systematically recording details relating to patients who were diagnosed with cancer. From 1971, as cancer treatment improved, and a greater percentage of patients recovered from cancer, regional cancer registries began to work together to collate a national cancer registry. This has allowed the NWTPS to analyse cancer incidence (as well as mortality) from when data became available in 1971.

The study guidelines state that information on the health of study participants is obtained only from the national records indicated above; it does not require specific examination of participants' body tissues. The study team will not seek to gain access to body tissues from participants or control group members.

This statement was deliberately inserted to hide the fact that we had records of deaths resulting from the nuclear testing programmes, and we know now that several of the participants in the tests died young and were never included in these figures.

Since 1983, the NRPB (now PHE) researchers have completed three full epidemiological analyses of the UK Participants in the UK Atmospheric Nuclear Weapons Tests and Experimental Programmes. The first epidemiological analysis was completed in 1988 and described the findings based on follow-up to 1983. A subsequent analysis, reported in 1993, described findings based on follow-up to 1990 and a third analysis, which considered follow-up to the end of 1998, was published in 2003. Each of these analyses was released by NRPB in a full report and also in a shorter paper which was published in a scientific journal (and as such was reviewed by independent scientists before publication).

The most recent publications were completed in 2004, when two review papers describing the NWTPS epidemiological studies and the results were published in the scientific Journal of Radiological Protection.

It was essential we ensured the MoD involvement in the studies was never disclosed. We initiated the report due to the concerns of the veterans and their families and as it was totally independent (as far as the public and the researchers knew) it would stand up in a court of law. The following statement was issued:

*"Researchers at PHE and its predecessor, the NRPB, are independent and do not work for the MoD. All of the researchers' reports have been published, in full, and additional papers have been published in respected peer-reviewed scientific journals. The reports and papers are written by the researchers and are not subject to MoD approval. In order to further demonstrate independence, the most recent analysis was overseen by an independent advisory group led by Professor Nicholas Wald, FRS."*

When reports are published in reputable scientific journals, those reports are first examined by independent experts who will provide a view on the reports, the findings and the work undertaken. If they think that the work has not been undertaken properly they will say so. This is called a peer-review process and such reputable journals will only publish papers which are accepted by the independent experts it consults. The three NWTPS analysis projects completed so far have been reported in two highly respected journals – the British Medical Journal, and the Journal of Occupational and Environmental Medicine.

What was unknown to the general public and the scientists who performed this study was that the list we gave them to work with did not contain the highest exposure personnel; we were instructed to give the NRPB the records of the personnel who had the least exposure. Other records were to be withheld and the NRPB were to be told that they were unavailable.

Only five members of my team, who had been selected specifically for the task of providing the information to the NRPB, knew the truth. We had hidden the most exposed people from the study and it was biased towards the British government from the start.

# Chapter 31 – Subjects with No Illness

In 1990, I was asked to attend a meeting of the NIA to discuss the possibility of finding healthy test subjects who had experienced no illnesses and had healthy, illness-free children. "We need to have evidence that personnel who participated in the tests have had no illness at all, no cancer treatments or any other medical problems," I was told. When I questioned the reason for finding such subjects, it was dismissed as a case study exercise. "We need to highlight these people."

I was to oversee the task, with members of the team searching through documentation to find subjects with no recorded problems.

It was during this exercise that computer database technology was becoming widely used within the government. As the task of finding personnel with no illness would take months, if not years, to complete manually, the decision was taken to computerise the records into a database which could be manipulated.

Our records were to be transferred and classified accordingly so that an indexing system could retrieve records in seconds, rather than taking hours of manual work.

This was a large undertaking; data operators were needed who had the appropriate clearance. It was decided that members of my team would be trained in the use of the database as they already had clearance.

The next 10 years were spent updating and collating the information into a database. This was Phase 3 of the project.

In 2000, the project was complete, and we had a fully functional database which could index and find personnel in seconds.

We performed our search of the database and found records of personnel who had no illness; either their records had not been updated or the records showed no issues.

These records were presented to the NIA board and I was tasked with investigating the small number of cases further to see if there had been any issues that had not been reported.

Of the 50 cases that I investigated, 10 men were dead; they had moved abroad to remote countries and our records were out of date. 15 had minor illnesses but no cancer-related incidents and the other 25 had issues with their children, grandchildren and great grandchildren.

Our records were becoming out of date and inaccurate. We needed to ensure that more effort was put into the monitoring of the personnel and with the new computer systems being introduced, we needed to ensure that the systems talked to each other automatically, rather than as a manual process.

# Chapter 32 – 2002: New Zealand Medal Award

A small group of veterans in New Zealand had been campaigning for several years under the leadership of Roy Sefton, who was a veteran of the Grapple tests. They were campaigning for a medal in recognition of their unique service to the government.

The New Zealand Nuclear Test Veterans Association had been created, similar in makeup to the British Nuclear Test Veterans Association, but smaller in number.

I was again summoned to a meeting to discuss the award of a medal. They were not asking for any compensation, just recognition of their contribution to the testing and the sacrifices made for the progression of nuclear technology.

It was debated at the meeting; the panel members were split as to whether to support such a medal. If we agreed to this medal award, then we may need to provide one for the British personnel as well.

As there were few of the New Zealand veterans left, it was decided that the NIA would support the application and would recommend that the New Zealand government should approve the award.

A delegation from the meeting approached the Queen and asked her to endorse the medal as head of the Commonwealth.

By now, the New Zealand government had adopted their own medal and awards system and broken away from the UK, so we had an excuse if the British veterans started a campaign. We could argue that they were completely independent, and that we had no control over their awards. Obviously, we did, as we had the evidence in the archives and had been heavily involved in the award approval process.

Two members of the panel wanted to give a UK version of this medal to the British Nuclear Test Veterans, with no liability, just a recognition of their service. This request was not supported by the board but was noted. I was one of the two who wanted to see the British veterans recognised by their own government.

Pressure was mounting from the various Associations across the world and as we were moving into a digital age, with people becoming more aware of their data, their data rights and requests under the new Freedom of Information Act 2000, we were moving into Phase 4 of our monitoring programme.

# Chapter 33 – Christmas Island Clean-up

In 2006/7, my team were asked to become involved in the clean-up of Christmas Island. The documents that we had now digitised were to be used to ascertain the areas where equipment and radioactive material had been dumped following the tests.

At the initial clean-up meeting of the NIA, the documents were reviewed, and the information used to co-ordinate a clean-up of materials and waste. The waste that needed to be removed would be brought back to the UK and placed in a landfill site in Teesside, Middlesbrough.

At this meeting, various discussions were held about why we were bringing the material back to the UK. The reasoning was if we were to bring it back, we could then show that the material was not radioactive and would not harm any personnel; we could use this to counter any arguments.

I then raised the question of why we were not contacting personnel who served on the island to help with the clean-up. Surely the people with the most knowledge of the scale of the clean-up were the people who had dumped the material in the first place.

This suggestion was immediately dismissed. The clean-up was to be undertaken with as little media attention as possible and we needed to ensure that the outcome was that the recovered material was of no harm to anyone either on the island or at the landfill site.

One junior official at the meeting asked a chilling question. "But what if we find radioactive material?" He was told that we wouldn't – and removed from the project. I never saw him again, at meetings or with any team involved in the test programme.

The clean-up went ahead as scheduled and documentary evidence of the material was secured by my team in the vaults at GCHQ. Material was taken to Middlesbrough and placed in landfill. In 2011, the local paper reported on the incident as follows:

*The Environment Agency approved the dumping at Port Clarence, Stockton, and said the only radioactive materials included in the load were luminous painted dials found in abandoned military vehicles. But* site operators Augean have admitted that they received 30 tonnes of radioactive sand from the Ministry of Defence.

Stockton North MP Alex Cunningham said he was "absolutely appalled" that the waste had been dumped on Teesside without the knowledge of the local community.

He called for the Ministry of Defence to explain why local people were not told that the waste was being dumped half a mile from the nearest residential area.

"I will be writing to the MoD to find out what has been going on here," he said. "I will also be seeking reassurances from the site about what exactly is dumped there and want them to prove to me and local people that this is not dangerous. If this is toxic waste, there must be all kinds of issues regarding safety.

"This kind of waste should not be dumped on a landfill in the middle of an unsuspecting community on Teesside."

Nine hydrogen bombs were detonated during tests by the British military at Christmas Island between 1956 and 1958.

Nearly 40 years later, the Government signed an agreement with the nation now known as the Republic of Kiribati to clear up the toxic waste left over. A total of 338 tonnes of the material was then transported more than 8,600 miles back to the UK and dumped at Port Clarence in 2008.

The Environment Agency, the MoD and Augean say the material only contains low levels of radioactivity and no threat is posed to the public.

But their initial statements on exactly what was included in the waste contradicted each other.

The MoD said that 338 tonnes of scrap metal, lead, asbestos and radioactive material was taken to the site.

Augean said that around 30 tonnes of sand with low levels of radioactivity was dumped there. The firm has today clarified that statement by saying it did process a total of 338 tonnes of waste, but only 30 of that was radioactive.

But the Environment Agency said that only luminous dials found in vehicles tested as radioactive, so the site was given approval to dump the material.

Dr David Lowry is a nuclear research specialist, and a member of the Nuclear Waste Advisory Associates group. He said: "The dials are meant to be the main radioactive hazard, but they detonated several large hydrogen bombs over Christmas Island. It's obvious that radioactive fallout came back onto the island.

"Why do they think the radioactive contamination from the bomb wasn't brought back to the UK?

"Why has this been approved to be put into landfill in a pretty densely populated area?

"What happens if the landfill gets flooded, and exempt material gets into the local streams and kids are fishing there? Would that be regarded as hazardous or not?"

A spokesman for Augean said that residents were not consulted because the waste was not considered to be hazardous enough to pose a risk.

He said that the material was transported to the site by the MoD in three lorries, and the sand was found to have "slightly elevated" levels of radioactivity. The exact route the lorries took is not known. He added: "I believe this would have been laid in the landfill and covered over almost immediately."

In a further statement today, the Environment Agency said the 30 tonnes of sand transported to Port Clarence was only radioactive because of the contact it had with the aluminised dials.

Environment manager Julian Carrington said: "The sand accepted by Port Clarence landfill was removed from the beach with the vehicle parts which lay on it.

"All this was tested before it left Kiribati and radioactivity present - at extremely low levels - was identified to have originated from painted dials from the military vehicles.

"Based on this information, the Environment Agency determined that these waste materials were suitable for disposal at Port Clarence landfill site."

*Kate Hudson, general secretary of the Campaign for Nuclear Disarmament said: "Whatever precautions are taken, dumping this within a residential area clearly presents a greater risk than disposing of it in a purpose-built isolated store."[3]*

Once again, the MoD and my department had managed to keep the radioactive material and the extent of the exposure a secret. It was, however, becoming increasingly difficult as social media and news articles were starting to appear on the Internet and the BNTVA had become a voice for the veterans and their claims.

---

[3] Teesside Gazette, 5 March 2011, updated 13 May 2013: https://www.gazette-live.co.uk/news/local-news/call-answers-over-nuclear-bomb-3684015

# Chapter 34 – Compensation Claims

Over the years, various compensation claims have been sought by the veterans. The first major case was in 1993. Two British veterans of Operation Grapple, Ken McGinley, a veteran of five of the tests, and Edward Egan, a veteran of Grapple Y, sued for £100,000 damages over multiple health problems which they attributed to their involvement in the tests.

They took their claim to the European Court of Human Rights, which rejected it in a 5-4 split decision on 9 June 1998.

An appeal to the court to re-open the case was declined in January 2000.

Documentary evidence to support their claim is held in the archives. It was withheld by the NIA, who claimed that if they paid out to the two veterans, potentially 22,000 other veterans would be eligible for compensation.

I was present at that meeting where it was decided to fight the case. The government was not prepared to admit any responsibility for the effects on the veterans and would, at any cost, fight them.

I was told by one senior official that if we kept fighting it, "eventually they will all be dead" and "the problem will go away by itself". But what about the descendants, I asked. He responded with: "Not our problem. They never witnessed the tests, so it's not an MoD issue."

I knew that the evidence was there, and I watched whilst the veterans fought for themselves and the other nuclear veterans across the world. They were never going to succeed; the British government had made its decision to fight them and had endless resources to ensure that they would win any case.

In March 2012, a group of 1,011 British ex-servicemen were denied permission to sue the UK Ministry of Defence by the Supreme Court, claiming too much time had elapsed since they became aware of their medical conditions, under the terms of the Limitation Act 1980. The MoD believed that this would be the last case. We had already fought two large cases and won both.

# Chapter 35 – War Pensions: Shirley Denson

In 2011, a war pension was awarded to the widow of a pilot who was forced to fly through the mushroom cloud. This award followed an appeal and, unfortunately for us, this was the first time that any documentary evidence had been had leaked through our systems and given to a member of the public.

The document contained dosimeter readings and evidence that her husband was used as a guinea pig in an 'experiment'.

In 2018, as part of the medal campaign, the following report appeared in the Daily Mirror.

*After more than 20 years of struggle she got a widow's war pension after finding proof that her late husband Eric had been irradiated while flying sampling missions during Britain's nuclear tests.*

*Eric had piloted a converted Canberra bomber "sniff" plane through the mushroom cloud of our biggest hydrogen bomb when it was detonated over Christmas Island in the South Pacific. But when he got home he started to have crippling headaches.*

*Shirley told me: "One day he was holding his head with tears running down his face. He was in agony. We took him to psychiatrists, but they had no idea what was wrong."*

*Twice Shirley found and saved her husband as he tried to commit suicide. The third time, in 1976, he succeeded, slashing his wrists in a wood near their home.*

*Shirley was told by the MoD all of his medical records during his time at Christmas Island have disappeared. But then she discovered a radiation meter in his cockpit registered a dose of 13 Roentgen - the equivalent of 12,000 dental X-rays.*

*Despite a series of legal hearings in which the MoD claimed Eric must have been mentally unstable because he used to wet the bed as a child, it was enough to win a war pension.*

*But Shirley didn't stop. After the Freedom of Information Act was passed she applied for further details of Eric's service. In December 2007 they sent her a single sheet of paper which confirmed his dose of*

13R, among the records of 13 other aircrew whose names and doses were blanked out.

And three months after that, they sent extra documents as "additional information".

It contained a bombshell.

There, in black and white, it said: "Thus the initial experiment was carried out on personnel flying the secondary sampler."

Eric's plane, codenamed Sniff Two, was the second to enter the cloud. Eric had been subjected to an experiment.

At the time veterans were trying to sue the MoD for negligence. Shirley gave their lawyers the documents, but as they had more than a million papers to read it seems to have been lost.

A little while ago she came across a copy and sent it on to me, because I've been reporting on the veterans' story for the past 16 years.

Like her, I've seen a lot of these old documents. This one was about testing the film radiation badges thousands of the veterans were given during the tests and comparing their readings to the "Charlie meter" which measured radiation in the cockpit.

I read through it, and then I fell off my chair.

"Experiment"! Blimey! Three paragraphs later: "Care was taken to ensure that as little shielding effect as possible was given by the ejector seat and that no equipment of any description shielded the badges."

I flicked back. For the test a badge was put behind each crew member's head, on his two arm rests, and on his seat pan. So, when they maximised radiation for the badges, they were maximising exposure of the men.

His dose according to the badge in the centre of his chest was 13R, as we already knew. But at the bottom of the page was this:

Figures derived from the four special P.M.3 badges

|  | Head | L. Arm rest | R. Arm rest | Seat pan |
|---|---|---|---|---|
| Pilot | 18.8 r | 12.5 r | 12.5 r | 8.8 r |
| Navigator | 17.0 r | 11.1 r | 11.0 r | 7.6 r |
| Wireless operator | 17.0 r | 10.7 r | 12.5 r | 7.6 r |

The dose to his head was the biggest of all - almost 19R. Could it *be linked to those headaches? And the specific dose to his testicles was 8.8R. You would need to work in a modern nuclear power station for about 460 years to get the same dose.*

*Eric has four generations of descendants. More than a third of them have an abnormality - including skull deformities, developmental problems, and extra and missing sets of teeth.*

*Eric knew he was flying through a mushroom cloud. He was likely aware of people testing these badges. But he wore no extra protection, and his widow is sure he was never told about a risk to his DNA.*

*Shirley said: "He never breathed a word about his missions to me, but if anyone had warned him about genetic damage he would never have let us have those children."*

*In February the chairman of the British Nuclear Test Veterans' Association, Alan Owen, told me four vets were returning to Christmas Island for the 60th anniversary of Grapple Y in April, and launching a medal campaign.*

*Mirror editor Alison Philips agreed to back it, and when a friend introduced me to Labour deputy leader Tom Watson I asked him to do the same. As a former defence minister, he knew of the issue, and had even tried to fix it by finding the scientific missing link the MoD had always demanded.*

*It requires scientific method that, geneticists say, has yet to be discovered.*

*But Tom was only in the job six months. Now, as deputy, he has some responsibility to talk about medal-giving, so said he'd throw his weight behind it. Veteran John Ward, 81, agreed to meet Tom in Parliament and talk to him about his experiences and his belief that they are to blame for his daughter Denise's extensive medical problems.*

*And then, with the greatest of pleasure, I rang the MoD.*

*I've rung them for comments a lot over the years. I usually have to explain to the press officer what nuclear veterans are before I explain the story.*

*"We've got a document from 1958 which says personnel were used in a radiation experiment," I said. "The only care taken was to ensure*

*they weren't shielded, and the scientists knew about the possibility of genetic damage. We're running it tomorrow."*

I emailed them the document. That was 9am on Tuesday morning. Over the course of the day the press office claimed the papers were just safety regulations, that it was an experiment on badges not men, and that policy documents say all kinds of stuff, so it wasn't to be believed. I pointed out, repeatedly, a pilot's radiation exposure was maximised despite official awareness he might have genetic damage, and this was no blue-sky policy idea but a scientific endeavour that actually happened.

An official comment landed in my inbox at 6pm.

It said veterans were welcome to apply for compensation and added: *"At the time the military monitored the health of our service personnel and it is no surprise that selected quotes from historical documents refer to this."*

The MoD has spent more than 30 years fighting every compensation and war pension claim brought by the veterans, at a cost to the public purse of more than £17m.

2. Monitoring their health? Really?

The Mirror decided to hold the story until the next day, in the hope of a comment that addressed the story. At 9am, I rang the MoD again. I pointed out the word *"monitor"* did not appear in the document once, while the word *"experiment"* featured prominently.

Off we went again. The press officer claimed this was evidence of keeping the men safe, and I pointed out Eric had zero protection while flying through a cloud produced by a bomb 100 times more powerful than that which levelled Hiroshima. The press officer went home, another started the evening shift, and a comment finally appeared at 8.30pm.

It said: *"It is not true to say that these men were subject to an experiment to look at the effects of radiation."*

I didn't say it was. I said Eric was USED in an experiment involving radiation - like he was a Bunsen burner, rather than a man. I note you don't deny it.

*"The British nuclear testing programme contributed towards keeping our country secure during the Cold War and regular health checks were conducted throughout."*

Where are the rest of Eric's records, then? You told Shirley you don't have any.

*"The National Radiological Protection Board has carried out three studies of nuclear test veterans and found no valid evidence to link participation in this programme to ill health."*

There's plenty of circumstantial evidence: studies have found 1 in 3 veterans had bone cancer or leukaemia, 3 times the normal rate of miscarriage, 10 times the usual number of birth defects, and elevated rates of infant death. And in 2011 a survey by THE MOD ITSELF found 83% of veterans had up to 10 different health conditions. It's just the MoD considers this evidence invalid.

We published the story on our front page on Thursday. Tom Watson went on Sky News to demand the Defence Secretary Gavin Williamson apologise to Shirley and reveal how many other nuclear veterans were involved in experiments. I did interviews on LBC, British Forces radio and Forces TV.

These are some of the messages I have had since from veterans and their families: "I had five sons after Christmas Island, they're all disabled"; "My nephew died aged 7 from leukaemia and my sister has an illness doctors cannot diagnose"; "My dad was at Grapple and I have extra teeth too".

And these, about the Mirror's splash yesterday: "About to go and buy the Mirror, I wish my dad could have seen this." And: "The front page! I was crying as I took it out of the stand. Dad died in 1983, still a young man, never knew his grandchildren."

Best of all, though, was a phone call from Shirley.

"Thank you, darling. You've done Eric proud, and told his story so well," she said. "Now, what can I do to help you next?"

And that's the bit Gavin Williamson should worry about. What will we do next?

Eric's story is undeniable, which is why the MoD press office spent

*35 hours coughing up a factual contortion, and he was one of dozens of aircrews. There were another 22,000 men on the ground facing different dangers. The hazards of radiation are well-known, and efforts are underway at Brunel University to find that scientific DNA link the MoD has so long demanded.*

*The veterans might be dying, but their children and their birth defects keep coming. The fallout isn't washing away but is instead growing more toxic the longer it is ignored.*

*And as long as there are people like Shirley - veterans, widows, children and grandchildren all determined to be an embuggerance for as long as it takes - the Defence Secretary had better keep his tin hat to hand.[4]*

So, the press had evidence that we had documents relating to the tests and the experiments carried out on the personnel. We needed to ensure that no further documents were released.

---

[4] Daily Mirror, 1 June 2018: https://www.mirror.co.uk/news/politics/how-you-find-proof-determined-12634090

# Chapter 36 – Infiltrating the BNTVA

The BNTVA now had branches across the UK and members across the world. We needed to find a way to infiltrate the board and ensure that everything they were planning would be fed back to the government.

We decided to look at the board and its trustees and see who we could use. This proved a difficult task until a civil servant was added to the board. We had a way in.

The BNTVA had now supported two compensation claims and numerous war pension claims and had finally won some. We were starting to lose control of the documentary evidence and we needed something that would stop the veterans from constantly campaigning.

The patron of the Association was a Member of Parliament and was the first person we needed to include in the plan. He was instructed to meet with the NIA and discuss the best way forward.

At the meeting, various discussions were held regarding the best way forward. Details of the US compensation programme were starting to filter through. There were also rumours that the Fijian government was proposing some compensation for their veterans.

We needed to ensure that the British government was seen to be co-operating with the veterans to ensure they did not begin any further campaigns.

It was decided that the best way forward was to propose a £25 million fund that would help with house adaptations and mobility items on a per veteran basis. The money would also be used for a DNA programme at Brunel University as a follow up to the 2005 Massey University study in New Zealand.

The MoD needed to control the DNA research and again hide the evidence. We could not allow for any findings using the new DNA techniques to prove that the veterans were exposed, even though we already knew it.

Meetings were held with two representatives of the BNTVA, including the civil servant. We did not want the board involved as it was to be another covert operation.

We had tapped the phones of the trustees for years, listening in to conversations, but this was the first time we had infiltrated the board.

In 2012, the United States passed the Radiation Exposure Compensation Act (RECA), a federal statute providing for the monetary compensation of people, including atomic veterans, who contracted cancer and a number of other specified diseases as a direct result of their exposure to atmospheric nuclear testing undertaken during the Cold War, or their exposure to radon gas and other radioactive isotopes while undertaking uranium mining, milling or the transportation of ore.

The Act provides the following remunerations:

- $50,000 to individuals residing or working 'downwind' of the Nevada Test Site
- $75,000 for workers participating in atmospheric nuclear weapons tests
- $100,000 for uranium miners, millers, and ore transporters

In all cases there are additional requirements which must be satisfied (proof of exposure, establishment of duration of employment, establishment of certain medical conditions, etc.).

Attempts to enact the legislation can be traced back to the late 1970s. In its fifth draft, a Bill entitled *Radiation Exposure Compensation Act of 1979* was sponsored by Senator Ted Kennedy of Massachusetts. The Bill intended to make compensation available to persons exposed to fallout from nuclear weapons testing and for living uranium miners (or their survivors) who had worked in Utah, Colorado, New Mexico and Arizona between 1 January 1947 and 31 December 1961.

The Bill proposed to pay compensation to persons who lived within prescribed areas for at least a year, to persons who "died from, has or has had, leukaemia, thyroid cancer, bone cancer or any other cancer identified by an advisory board on the health effects of radiation and uranium exposure".

Fallout areas listed by the Bill included counties in Utah and Nevada. Utah counties included Millard, Sevier, Beaver, Iron, Washington, Kane, Garfiend, Piute, Wayne, San Juan, Grand, Carbon,

Emery, Duchesne, Uintah, San Pete and Juab. Nevada's 'affected areas' were listed as the counties of White Pine, Nye, Lander, Lincoln and Eureka. The Bill as drafted, would have also compensated ranchers whose sheep died following nuclear weapons tests "Harry" (13 May 1959) and "Nancy" (24 May 1953).

Twelve years transpired before a similar bill was finally enacted, which added to the list uranium miners who worked in Wyoming and extended the eligible date rate for employed miners to between 1947 and 1971. In the successful bill it was written that Congress "apologizes on behalf of the nation" to individuals who were "involuntarily subjected to increased risk of injury and disease to serve the national security interests of the United States."

It was initially expected that hundreds of compensation claims would be paid under the Act, a figure which later proved to be a gross underestimate.

The Radiation Exposure Compensation Act was passed by Congress on October 5, 1990 and signed into law by President George H. W. Bush on October 15.

In some cases, it proved to be extremely difficult for people to receive their compensation, including cases filed by widows of uranium miners. Because many uranium miners were Native Americans, they did not have standard marriage licenses required to establish a legal connection to the deceased. In 1999, revisions were published in the Federal Register to assist in making award claims. Many mine workers and their families found the paperwork difficult and qualifications narrow and were declined compensation.

In 2000, additional amendments were passed which added two new claimant categories (uranium mill and ore workers, both eligible to receive as much money as uranium miners), added additional geographic regions to the 'downwind' provisions, changed some of the recognized illnesses, and lowered the threshold of radiation exposure for uranium miners.

In 2002, additional amendments were passed as part of another bill, primarily fixing a number of draftsmanship errors in the previous amendments (which had accidentally removed certain geographic areas from the original act) and clarified a number of points.

In order to be eligible for compensation, an affected uranium industry worker must have developed lung cancer, fibrosis of the lung, pulmonary fibrosis, cor pulmonale related to fibrosis of the lung, or silicosisor pneumoconiosis following their employment. In the case of uranium mill workers and ore transporters, renal cancer and chronic renal disease were also compensable conditions.

As of 20 April 2018, 34,372 claims in total had been approved with total compensation paid at $2,243,205,380.

The NIA monitored these figures and calculated there was the potential for 22,000 claims for compensation from veterans and their family members. If 22,000 claims for £75,000 were to be filed under any UK compensation programme, the bill would amount to £1,650,000,000 a figure that the British government could not afford.

Regular meetings were held to discuss the compensation and it was decided that insufficient funds were available to meet the potential demand for compensation. Instead, an operation codenamed NCCF would be undertaken and £25 million allocated to a fund for veterans. This was considerably lower than the estimates of potential compensation claims.

# Chapter 38 – Fujian Compensation

In January 2015, the Prime Minister of Fiji, Frank Bainimarama, announced that the Fijian government would provide Fiji $9,855 (US $4,788) in compensation payments to those Fijian servicemen who had participated in Operation Grapple. This payment would only be made to those who had survived and as the numbers were very low, the 24 men received the full amount.

It was at this time that the NIA again debated giving small amounts of compensation to the surviving British personnel, of which there were two thousand. This led to discussions relating to the widows, war pension claims, surviving families and the Massey study.

The government could be looking at billions if we admit liability. The cost of administering such a scheme, the pay-outs and the legal challenges would cripple our already stretched budgets.

It was at this meeting that I presented a document from a previous NMC meeting where the cost of paying compensation in the 1980s was estimated at £20 million, not billions. Perhaps we made the wrong decision, I proposed.

The monitoring process, my team's salaries and the cost of fighting legal claims had already topped the £400 million mark. If we had come clean in the 1980s, we could have saved millions if not billions of pounds.

Because of my opinion, I was seen as an old man who was living in the past. One new member of the NIA even referred to me as a "dinosaur" who had not kept up with technology, advances in science and the digital age.

I reminded him that we had evidence that we had exposed these men. "We did it," I said. "We used these men as guinea pigs, exposed them, monitored them and have caused their families so much distress." If he had witnessed the deceit and lies first hand, I am sure he would have a different outlook.

The meeting concluded that the best way forward was still to set up a fund to allow veterans to be supported in their later years; there was no liability, just money to help. It was the cheapest option and the easiest way to stop the growing campaigns of the British nuclear test veterans.

In 2018, the French government announced that they would be paying compensation to their nuclear participants. This was a major step forward for Aven, who represented the French veterans.

The UK refused to acknowledge any damage had been caused and become the only major super power at the nuclear table not to compensate their veterans, even though other countries who had been present at the same tests as the UK had acknowledged the sacrifices of their personnel.

Further meetings were held with the BNTVA's patron and representatives. It was made very clear that the award of this £25 million would go to the nuclear veterans and would include a DNA programme at Brunel University which would be controlled by the NIA.

The patron was to use his position as an MP to lobby the government on behalf of the BNTVA, even though the money had already been agreed. A plan was put into action to ensure that it was the best that the BNTVA could do. The award of the money would bring relief to the remaining veterans and their families if they needed help.

A co-ordinated plan was drawn up between the NIA and the BNTVA to promote the campaign. Once it was announced, other veterans' organisations campaigned for a share of the money, something which was not envisaged at the time. An emergency meeting was held.

The British government could not be seen to be giving £25 million to the nuclear veterans and not supporting other veteran charities; it would show that we had prioritised the nuclear veterans and co-ordinated a plan. We needed a cover story, so the 'Aged Veterans Fund' was created. This organisation would receive applications from the veterans' charities for a portfolio of projects and would review and award the monies where necessary.

More money was needed if we were to award the full £25 million to the BNTVA. Unfortunately, following many discussions, it was agreed that the money would be split amongst all the charities, with the BNTVA receiving £6 million of the original £25 million.

A compromise was drawn up between the NIA and the then chairman of the BNTVA. He was to stand down as chairman and set up a company to manage the fund, of which he would become the portfolio manager. For this he could claim 10% in management fees to run the portfolio of projects, including the DNA programme. For the initial project term of four years across two phases, he would be able to earn £400,000 from the programme. He would also receive an MBE for his services. He immediately resigned from the BNTVA and started his company, but remained as a special advisor to the board and the other BNTVA representative was appointed chairman. We now had full control over both the charity and the portfolio manager and his company.

The government would handle any fallout from this and would ensure that due diligence had been completed and that any conflicts of interest were dismissed. It was agreed by the representatives that they would take the offer. We had effectively ended the campaigning years of the BNTVA – or so we thought.

Two representatives were enlisted to ensure that the BNTVA and their members were informed that they would receive help for adaptations, help to travel to events, and that remembrance stones across the country would be re-dedicated and repaired. With the DNA project cost of £2 million, it would once and for all prove that DNA had been damaged by the tests.

The project was underway. Little did the membership of the BNTVA know that the NIA were controlling the project and its findings. Phase 5 of our monitoring programme was now underway.

Various rounds of the Aged Veterans Fund applications were undertaken, and grants awarded. The two representatives had effective control of £6 million and needed to implement the second phase of the NCCF project by setting up a new charity separate from the BNTVA which would control the funds. This was achieved in September 2017, when the NCCF and BNTVA divorced themselves from each other. We believed that this would be the end of the BNTVA as memberships were dwindling and the number of veterans and their families had effectively given up on any recognition or compensation. Applications to the NCCF would be enough to satisfy the remaining veterans.

We continued to monitor both organisations through our representatives as the new company set up by the previous chairman was also providing services to the BNTVA – which allowed us to look at emails and documents.

# Chapter 40 – BNTVA Medal Campaign

Our plan was working very well. Veterans had applied for help and a reunion in Weston Super Mare in September 2017 was fully funded by the NCCF. The veterans were happy.

Then stories started to emerge from veterans who were not happy that the ex-chairman was receiving so much money from the fund. Veterans were told that small grants claims had been withdrawn and that no overseas visits would be funded, the help to events also stopped and was not to be resurrected.

This was after a delegation had attended a French 'rekindling of the flame' ceremony at which the chairman of the NCCF had relit the flame. It was an all-expenses paid trip financed by the NCCF; it seemed as if the NIA had created a monster who was now using the fund for their own personal gain.

OBSIVEN is an organisation who work to co-ordinate the efforts of nuclear charities across the world. Our contact, who we had paid off, was now the president of OBSIVEN UK and was using NCCF money to promote the charity via a new magazine.

Our plan was starting to crack; we needed urgent action. The ex-trustees of the BNTVA were starting to ask questions about finances, how the award had happened, why grants had stopped.

The new chairman of the BNTVA was present on the NCCF board and the Brunel University board. We needed to have him removed without delay; he could not be allowed to see any details of our projects or their outcomes.

Following a meeting with the two ex-BNTVA representatives who were now running the NCCF, it was decided that a complaint should be made against the chair which would be upheld, resulting in his removal from the NCCF board, thus removing him from the advisory board as well.

This plan was executed and completed in February 2018. However, he remained as the chairman of the old BNTVA, but as this charity was being shut down, there was nothing to worry about.

We then received a call from the chairman of the NCCF who had received a report from a senior official of the Aged Veterans Fund stating that the old BNTVA still had responsibility for the grants rather than the NCCF; he had written to the BNTVA to inform them. We had a serious problem. If this was the case, then the old charity could not be closed down; it would need to remain, and the old trustees would want to be re-instated.

The chairman of the NCCF was tasked with forcefully removing the chairman of the BNTVA via a meeting held to an agenda decided by the NIA. This took place in July 2018 and the chairman was duly removed.

Our plan was working well, and we had no legal claims, campaigns or issues to worry about. We now had full control of both the NCCF and the DNA programme.

At the BNTVA Annual Conference in Weston Super Mare in 2018, the chairman announced that they would be campaigning for a medal. They had secured a partnership with the Daily Mirror for exclusive rights and would be campaigning for recognition, using Shirley Denson as the main piece, along with Douglas Hern, who had campaigned for justice for years.

Despite our best efforts, all our plans to stop the campaigning of the charity had come to nothing. Another phase was starting but this time the nuclear test veterans' descendants had taken the helm. We could no longer rely on our contacts within the organisation and we had no contact with any of the trustees. We needed a way forward.

As we had removed the BNTVA trustees from the NCCF board, it was decided that we should offer the chairman trusteeship again, even though the fictitious complaint had been upheld by the board and he had been asked to leave. The NCCF chairman asked the BNTVA chairman if he would re-join the NCCF as a trustee. He declined.

To add to matters, the evidence produced by the Daily Mirror in 2011 to assist with Shirley Denson's war pension application was being used again. This document was still the only evidence that had been released to the public and could lead to the floodgates being opened.

An online petition was started, and the signatures soon came in. Veterans appeared on Sky News, in national newspapers, on regional news and on the radio. The campaign was starting to build momentum, not least because the comedian Al Murray was backing it. The National Association of Atomic Veterans in the USA and the New Zealand Nuclear Veterans Association all backed the campaign.

The patron was told to step down from his role with the BNTVA and instead become patron of the NCCF, as he was part of the Aged Veterans Fund setup. He quickly drew up his resignation. In his place, John Hayes became patron of the BNTVA and backed the campaign, with the support of Tom Watson (deputy leader of the Labour party).

The veterans' descendants had taken on the fight for their fathers. Susie Boniface, who was an independent journalist, was pushing the campaign and calling the MoD on a regular basis.

The issue was raised during Prime Minister's Questions and during the Defence Secretary's questions. More and more MPs were supporting the campaign for the medal and a launch day was held at the Houses of Parliament.

We had a problem.

We needed a plan to ensure that the evidence we held was not disclosed. We could not allow any further documents to be released.

An emergency meeting of the NIA was held in London.

It was decided that the Defence Secretary (Gavin Williamson) would meet with representatives of the veterans, Shirley Denson, John Hayes and the Chairman of the BNTVA to discuss their campaign and the response from the MoD. This was to be scheduled as soon as possible so that any further requests from veterans via their MPs could be answered with a letter stating that a meeting was to take place.

The outcome of the meeting was to be as follows:

1. A new NRPB study was to be undertaken to include the families of the veterans.

2. A sub-committee would be set up to look at new evidence and review the 2012 medal review, when it was decided that the nuclear veterans would not be eligible for a medal.

3. The medals and awards committee would review the findings and, if in agreement, would put forward a medal for signoff by the queen.

This would allow the remaining veterans to receive recognition. The cost to the government would be relatively small compared to paying billions in compensation and, with the NCCF funds, would allow the nuclear veterans to die knowing that their service had been recognised.

The meeting was held at Whitehall in July 2018. All parties were happy with the outcome and as I write, committees are being formed and the review is being undertaken.

I can reveal that the decision has already been made by the NIA. Mounting pressure to reveal further documents from our vault and the low costs involved in medal production has meant that the veterans will finally be awarded with a medal and will receive recognition for the roles they played.

The awarding of this medal will demonstrate that the MoD does care about their serviceman and that they recognise their sacrifice. That will be the official statement.

The online petition has now reached the 10,000 mark and we had to respond. the NIA wrote an official statement for the MoD, which was as follows:

*The government continues to recognise and be grateful to all service personnel and civilians who participated in the British nuclear testing programme.*

*Their selfless contribution ensured that the UK was equipped with the deterrent we needed during the dangerous years of the Cold War.*

*The Ministry of Defence has asked the Cabinet Office if The Committee on the Grants of Honours, Decorations and Medals (The HD Committee) would consider looking afresh at the previous information, and examine any new evidence presented by campaigners. If the Committee decides that a medal is appropriate recognition for veterans, a recommendation will be made to Her Majesty The Queen. It is envisaged that if the recommendation is supported any subsequent medal*

*would be made available to all those who witnessed the nuclear tests.*
    *Ministry of Defence*

I am happy that these veterans will finally receive their recognition. In my view it is 60 years too late and it has taken too much fighting, too much deceit, too many lies and covert operations to get to this stage. I refer back to my document from the 1980s when we decided not to admit any responsibility. It's was one of the biggest mistakes in British government history.

Maybe one day the government will accept responsibility for their actions, but I doubt it. After spending my whole professional life protecting these secrets and the covert operations that were undertaken, there will never be a full release of these files.

# Chapter 41 – The End of My Life

You are now up to date with the NIA involvement in the British nuclear testing programme. The lies and level of deceit may seem unbelievable to some of you – it sounds like the plot of a James Bond movie – but I can assure you that it is true.

I am not proud of my role in this cover-up. Thousands of people have died, families are suffering, and people have committed suicide because of the levels of radiation they were exposed to.

For years, I have felt the guilt of the monitoring, which has taken place for over 60 years; the lies and deceit; and my betrayal of these servicemen, who knew nothing of their exposure.

A number of people have come close to uncovering the truth, and a number have been paid off to ensure that the veterans do not continue to fight for justice.

The British government has spent millions of pounds on clean-ups, compensation to the Tjarutja people, compensation to the Fijians. The American government has a compensation scheme and the French have just introduced a scheme.

But the British government would rather fight the veterans. I estimate the cost to the British government is over £200 million in salaries, computer systems and the monitoring of the veterans. £12 million alone has been spent fighting the veterans in court – veterans who are only trying to claim war pensions and receive some recognition from the government for the role they played. The BNTVA's new medal campaign is exceptional. 'Still engaging an invisible enemy' is a great tagline and the logo, videos and campaign material being produced are fantastic

At the time of writing, our database shows that there are 1,345 personnel left who were present at the tests. By 2050, when our project is due to finish, there will be none left. Perhaps then the truth will be exposed by their descendants – but I doubt it.

The secrets of the testing programme will likely never be uncovered. The British government will never accept responsibility for what they did to these poor men, who became human guinea-pigs for their entire lives, their families suffering every day. We thought we were monitoring 22,000 personnel. We are now monitoring over 150,000 descendants. We do not want them to come together and voice their opinions.

The evidence is out there: I have it stored in a secure area. The government knows nothing about this. Whilst the information was being transferred to the database, files were delivered to my house in South Wales, where they were copied and stored securely. They are not digitised; they are the original paper files that contain damming evidence of the tests, the monitoring process and the 100-year experiment.

I have entrusted the location of these files with two men, and the storage costs have been paid for until 2060.

In the event of my death, these files will be sent to the Daily Mirror for the attention of Susie Boniface, who has campaigned tirelessly for the veterans and is helping to ensure that their latest medal campaign is covered in the press. I wish her well with the documents and hope that the evidence she has been hoping to find will be finally delivered to her, this horrible experiment will no longer be a secret – and the truth will finally be exposed.

# Addendum by Slaine McRoth

It is with great sadness that I must inform you that on 1 July 2018, Sir James Gordon Josephson died at home, alone, of lung cancer.

His final wish for the documents to be exposed could not be completed as a fire in the storage area where they were being stored has destroyed them.

He took every precaution in storing the documents, even sending them abroad to ensure their safety, but unfortunately this tragic end means the claims in this book cannot be justified. It is strange that, only two days after his death, the documents were destroyed. Perhaps the influence of the NIA was such that, even in his last few days, they managed to retrieve the secret location.

On 3 July, the storage facility in Santa Rosa, California, USA suffered serious fire damage. This report is from The Press Democrat:

*Fire broke out at a large Santa Rosa Avenue storage facility early Tuesday, causing at least $500,000 in damages, fire officials said.*

*The two-alarm fire destroyed or damaged personal belongings in as many as 30 storage units at the U-Haul Moving & Storage just after 6 a.m., said Cyndi Foreman, investigator and fire prevention officer for Rincon Valley and Windsor fire districts. The cause still remains under investigation, but candles may have sparked the fire in a downstairs storage unit, she said.*

*Foreman, who led the investigation, said the renter of the burned unit had been at the facility Monday evening and used a candle for lighting as the storage units have no power, she said.*

*She also couldn't rule out the possibility someone discarded a cigarette in the unit.*

*Dispatchers received 911 calls from several people, including a property manager who had arrived at work to find smoke coming out the front of the two-story building.*

*The facility, which is just north of Todd Road and butts up against Highway 101, has 60 storage units.*

*Rincon Valley firefighters arrived first and found thick black*

*smoke coming from the front entrance and spreading through the roof,
said Santa Rosa Fire Battalion Chief Ken Sebastiani, who led the firefight.*

*The nearest hydrant was about 1,000 feet away, fire officials said.
With the fire threatening the other storage units, they called for additional firefighters and water.*

*Thick black smoke and a long row of locked doors made it difficult
to determine the fire's location, Foreman said.*

*"The crews had their work cut out for them," she said. "There
were heavy steel doors that had to be breached and they had to cut
locks on dozens of units to be sure we didn't have any hidden fire."*

*The fire started in a 10-by-12-foot unit in the centre of the building,
fire officials said. Firefighters contained the flames to the unit, but
smoke and heat damaged adjoining units and likely ruined items in the
rest of the downstairs storage rooms, Foreman said.*

*Some smoke got into the second floor, but those 30 units appeared
undamaged, she said.*

*"It could have gone up exponentially if they'd not had a handle on
this and preserved the second floor," Foreman said, referring to firefighters.*

*Investigators will review video surveillance footage from the
building. The fire doesn't appear to be suspicious, she said.*[5]

It has been my great pleasure to write this book for Sir James. He was
a great man who was dedicated to his work. There were many times in
his life when he wanted to expose the experiments, but he decided to
leave it until his death to ensure that the British nuclear test veterans'
voice would be heard.

I wish I could end this book with reports of the veterans receiving
justice and compensation for their exposure during the tests. Unfortunately, I cannot. Perhaps in 2050 – or when the last veteran dies – we

---

[5]     https://www.pressdemocrat.com/news/8497814-181/2alarm-fire-damages-santa-
rosa?sba=AAS

will see these documents exposed.

Why the British government has decided to fight these veterans is not known. The cost of paying compensation – like the American government has – would be significantly lower.

I firmly believe the new BNTVA, with the descendants at the helm, will continue the fight. The British government got it wrong, and if they believe the problem will go away once the last veteran dies, they're wrong. The determination of the veteran's descendants is stronger than ever.

As a country, we need to honour these veterans, give them a medal, pay the compensation, and give them war pensions without an argument. As the BNTVA says, they are still fighting an invisible enemy. Well, I can tell them that they are still fighting the British government – and they must not stop. Keep going: as the TV series 'The X-Files' says, "The truth is out there."

# References

Where information was not available, Wikipedia has been used to ensure that the information is as correct as possible.

This book has largely been drawn from content from the following Wikipedia pages:

*https://en.wikipedia.org/wiki/Operation_Grapple*

*https://en.wikipedia.org/wiki/Maralinga*

*https://en.wikipedia.org/wiki/Nuclear_weapons_and_the_United_Kingdom*

*https://en.wikipedia.org/wiki/Radiation_Exposure_Compensation_Act*

*https://en.wikipedia.org/wiki/Christmas_Island_(disambiguation)*

*https://en.wikipedia.org/wiki/Limitation_Act_1980*

*https://en.wikipedia.org/wiki/Kiritimati*

*https://en.wikipedia.org/wiki/British_nuclear_tests_at_Maralinga*

*https://en.wikipedia.org/wiki/McClelland_Royal_Commission*

*https://en.wikipedia.org/wiki/Lorna_Arnold*

*https://en.wikipedia.org/wiki/Operation_Dominic*

*https://en.wikipedia.org/wiki/Maralinga:_Australia%27s_Nuclear_Waste_Cover-up*

*https://en.wikipedia.org/wiki/Cobalt-60*

*https://en.wikipedia.org/wiki/Emu_Field,_South_Australia*

*https://en.wikipedia.org/wiki/Operation_Totem*

*https://en.wikipedia.org/wiki/Operation_Mosaic*

*https://en.wikipedia.org/wiki/Blue_Danube_(nuclear_weapon)*

*https://en.wikipedia.org/wiki/Nuclear_weapons_and_the_United_Kingdom#First_test_and_early_systems*

*https://en.wikipedia.org/wiki/Montebello*

25968295R00084

Printed in Great Britain
by Amazon